Passing Game

PASSING GAME

Christopher Brookhouse

Safe Harbor Books
NEW LONDON, NEW HAMPSHIRE
2000

ISBN: 0-9665798-2-8

Library of Congress Card Number: 00-190466

Passing Game
is a work of fiction. Any resemblance of its characters
to people living or dead is coincidental.

Christopher Brookhouse is the author of three novels and two
collections of poetry. One of his novels, *Running Out*, won
the Rosenthal Award from the American Academy of Arts and Letters.

Frontispiece photograph courtesy of *The Boston Globe*.
Author photograph © 2000 by Suki Coughlin.

Other books by Christopher Brookhouse:

FICTION
Running Out
Wintermute
Dear Otto

POETRY
Scattered Light
The Light Between the Fields

ONE

THE LETTER FROM Philip Pratt to Presley Alston begins, *Presley, I loved you long before I loved your sister.*

Even now, years later, despite what we were and what we have become, moments we shared whisper to me, a song one hears a few bars of and can't put out of mind until the song has played to the end again.

The first time I saw you, you were sitting in your father's car in the sunshine. I had passed my Harvard entrance exam. I was carrying my suitcase along Massachusetts Avenue toward the Yard. My friend Jimmy Rosen had taken the morning off from the messenger service to help me move into the room in Thayer. One suitcase was all I had, not enough to need Jimmy's help; but Jimmy, whom you met once on an evening you probably count as one of the worst in your life, enjoyed going places he said he didn't belong. Harvard Yard was one of those.

We stopped for a lemonade. Jimmy and I were joking about the uniforms we wore in the messenger service, our little hats with numbers on them, and the times he would have a message to deliver at one of the department stores and pretend to be lost so he could try to peek into the women's changing rooms.

We finished our lemonades and came out to the street. An open car waited at the curb. Your father had gone into Leavitt & Pierce to buy cigars. You were sitting in the car. Your suit coat fit your shoulders so well. Sleeves the right length. Your cuff links gleamed in the sun. Two women walked past. They blushed and giggled. You must have winked at them. Or blown them a kiss.

Your father appeared and cast his eyes over me and stepped into the car. What about one more anonymous young man whose clothes didn't fit very well, who was carrying his possessions in one battered suitcase like a refugee, was memorable? He might have remembered Jimmy, though, his Jewish looks. His parents had been real refugees.

I saw you other times too, mostly around the Yard, or sometimes having a coffee in Billings & Stover, always with someone dressed as well as you, someone who lived on Mt. Auburn Street, the Gold Coast crowd. Yet you didn't appear to care for their company as much as they cared for yours. That impressed me. The person you really appreciated was Humphrey. Humphrey, clumsy and inept, the kind of chubby boy who was the butt of jokes at his prep school, who had too much money and no talent for much besides consuming cocktails and making foolish passes at handsome women.

The first time you spoke to me was one late-summer day our sophomore year. I stood in front of the bulletin board near the locker room hoping to find my name on the list for second varsity. You were reading over my shoulder. You'd already found your own name on the list of firsts. Play a year of class football, you said. You'll end up on the team.

You never introduced yourself and I was surprised you knew my name. When I turned around, you were already disappearing through the door, vanishing into the sunlight.

The next time you said, See, I was right. Junior year. My name was on the list of firsts. Presley Alston, you said. We shook hands. Philip Pratt, I said. You smiled. Perfect teeth. I'd hardly ever been to a dentist until the Army sent me to one. My father was rather forgetful about such things.

You predicted before the season is over I'd be a starter. Coach Haughton started me in the Yale game. We didn't win but the writers praised my blocking and your running. After the game, I saw you get into a car. A woman was leaning against the seat. She wore evening clothes and was smoking a cigarette. Women always liked you, I heard someone say.

We didn't speak to each other again until we boarded the truck the next spring to be transported to Fresh Pond to march and learn to fire rifles and how to flag signals and how to charge between the rows of sandbags and bayonet imaginary Germans. We were wearing uniforms President Lowell arranged for us to receive. Old ones. Spanish-American War. He didn't want us training to be soldiers without uniforms. Yours fit you perfectly.

Wilson declared war in April. In May you invited me to the Hounds. You explained the club rule: A man could be a guest only once in his life. Might as well be now, you said. We were going to France and might not come back alive. I had a lot to drink and went outside and necked with a woman I had just met. I met Humphrey that night. I understand why you play football, he said. I don't understand why Presley does.

Humphrey meant I was poor and must be used to brawling the way the Irish players were or players from Italian families. When I asked you, you said you were good at football and you liked what you were good at. What about me? you asked. I said everyone in the little school in Charleston I attended was required to play one sport a year to build body and character. I didn't say I chose football because of the uniform. I could put it on and cover my head with a helmet and hide. A masquerade with cuts and bruises. But I could run well, run fast. I didn't get roughed up very much.

Once Lily asked if there wasn't another reason I kept playing after we'd come back from the war and were so much older and different from the rest of the team. She was referring to the race thing. She was right. She was right about you too. In prep school you played against people like yourself, from the same background and culture; but the colleges were bringing in the players Humphrey referred to, the Italians and the Irish. You wanted to prove a life of privilege didn't make you weak.

We took your integrity for granted. You looked the part. Your wide shoulders, your perfect teeth, your smooth skin, your blue eyes, your sandy hair parted in the middle. A recruiting poster for New England stock. Your family had been soldiers and statesmen. Your future in the diplomatic service was assured. On the boat going over to France, how quickly the senior officers respected you and deferred to your opinions. Captain Connors liked you right away. You were the one who discovered the cook who tried to betray our position. You were the one who punished him. You would have taken care of Devon too. Poor Devon, tied to a stake in his garden.

⁂

Pratt leaned on his elbow, bent closer to the lamp flame to light a cigarette. Nearby, on the ground above them, a German 77 exploded, blowing up more of the muddy French landscape, another crater for the rain to fill and some unlucky soldier to stumble into in the dark.

Pratt and Alston had the dugout to themselves. The French had made it, thirty feet under the ground. The French were good at building dugouts, dry and reasonably comfortable ones. But in a couple of days the men expected to receive orders to change position and follow the infantry, pushing the Germans back.

Captain Connors had been gassed a week earlier and couldn't open his eyes. Alston, a lieutenant, was in charge now. Pratt commanded the horse line, but there had been too many casualties near the guns. Pratt had put a corporal in charge of the horses and taken over the caissons bringing up the ammunition, helping to pass it hand to hand to the soldiers in the ammunition pits. In another hour Pratt would ascend the ladder to stand watch in case the infantry fired a flare. Green for gas alert. The battery was down too many men to lose any more like Captain Connors.

Pratt put out his cigarette and lay back. He remembered the smirk on Connors's face when he encountered Pratt and the woman walking down the hill from Montmartre. He remembered the way Connors bowed.

"Are you thinking about football?" Alston asked.

Pratt edged Connors out of mind. "Paris," Pratt answered.

"You're going to play again, aren't you?"

"Assuming the Germans don't kill us first."

"They're only guessing where we are."

"If the weather clears, they'll send the planes up."

"As long as we don't give ourselves away shooting at them, we'll be all right."

Another shell exploded close by, rattling the cots. "The guesses are getting better."

"Luck," Alston said.

Pratt started thinking about Connors again.

Pratt and Alston had met Connors on the boat coming over, a converted liner that sailed from New York one foggy night on a course for Halifax, then fourteen days across the open sea. The officers had the staterooms and the rest of the battery were in second class. Connors came from St. Louis and attended officers training school in Plattsburg. Pratt and Alston had enrolled in the R.O.T.C. program and trained at Fresh Pond on the outskirts of Cambridge under the disabled French officers President Lowell of Harvard had invited to the college.

After arriving in France the regiment was quartered in an abandoned village in the country, where they practiced setting up and loading their guns. One of the officers Pratt and Alston knew at Harvard arranged for them to spend some days in Paris. Connors managed to talk his way into going along.

The woman wore a floppy hat that hid most of her face. She had stopped Pratt by a row of linden trees. She spoke a little English. She said she'd show Pratt around. She knew some nice places to eat and drink, cheerful spots, reminders of the real Paris before the Germans sent over zeppelins to drop bombs and the city lights were blued and covered with tin bonnets.

May I present Annette, Pratt said on the steps down the hill from Montmartre. Annette held out her hand to Connors, but he didn't take it. Pleased to meet you, he said and bowed courteously, too courteously, Pratt thought, but he wouldn't take her hand. Had he done so, Pratt might not have felt the way he did. He wasn't naive. He realized Annette would invite him to her room somewhere. It turned out to be in a small hotel near the Gare St. Lazare. He intended to decline her invitation. But when Connors refused to touch her hand, Pratt changed his mind. He understood what someone not touching you was like. He ended up going to the small hotel near the Gare St. Lazare with Annette. Lying beside her, he told her what he'd never told anyone else. Why not? He would never see her again.

Connors went on down the hill. He didn't much care for Pratt. Too withdrawn and serious for his taste. Perhaps a bit common. Not at all in the image of a Harvard man as he took form in Connors's imagination. Alston, however, fit the image perfectly. Alston liked to drink and laugh, a good club man. He stood tall and strong in his new uniform and puttees. Blueness filled his eyes. Connors figured that Alston would never be tempted by someone like the woman in the floppy hat, a woman whose skin smelled like flowers, too many flowers, as if she doused herself in perfume to hide the way she really smelled. Yet he granted her a certain charm.

Several shells exploded almost simultaneously. The earth shook. Dirt fell between the cracks in the boards overhead. Pratt stood up and brushed his hand over his shirt.

"Just luck you think?" Pratt said angrily.

"What do you think?"

"I'll tell you tomorrow," Pratt said, and climbed the ladder.

Another shell exploded, but not close enough to concern him. At first he had not been afraid of dying, only of not being a good soldier. Their last evening in Paris he and Alston had dined together at the Hôtel de Crillon and afterward strolled in the Place de la Concorde among the pale statues. Pratt said, I want to be as good as you are; and Alston answered, What makes you think I'll be a good soldier? Because you come from a tradition of it, Pratt replied. You'll do fine, Alston said; I'll kick your ass if you don't. You and Coach Haughton, Pratt said, and both men laughed.

After their walk among the statues, Pratt had said good night. He wished to be by himself. Alston didn't. He stopped at the Ritz for a drink. Connors was there with a couple of other men and three women. Connors was glassy-eyed and almost asleep. A floppy hat hid part of the face of the woman beside Connors.

Time for bed, one of the men suggested. They stood up and helped Connors out of the bar. The woman in the hat said something in French, something too colloquial for Alston to make sense of it. The other women laughed. Annette, you are too cruel, one of them remarked.

May I see you home? Alston asked. The woman in the hat looked up in surprise, happy the evening wouldn't be a total waste.

The Americans Annette had been with all seemed in a hurry or they wanted to question her about her life. It pleased them if she said they were brave to come to France to fight or complimented their manhood. Alston was different. He didn't watch her undress as if he had never seen a woman take her clothes off before, curious and embarrassed at the same time. Instead he appraised her. She noted his approval. Then he told her what to do, what he liked. He pleased her well enough too.

Later, while she smoked a cigarette, she mentioned an American missing a toe. Some men took it off, the man had explained to her. She made a chopping gesture with the edge of her hand. I asked why, she said, and he said they could have cut off something else. She pronounced the words slowly, but it took Alston a minute to understand her. His friend Pratt was missing a toe. He was self-conscious about it and usually kept a sock on. Well, all sorts of people were missing toes, Alston thought. The streets of London and Paris were full of men missing lots of parts. Soon the streets of New York and Boston and Philadelphia and everywhere else would be full of men missing toes and hands and feet and arms.

Annette laughed. With me it didn't matter though. He didn't use what he had, she said. She rubbed her palm up Alston's thigh.

Before Alston left, he placed some money on the dresser. Quite a bit of money, she calculated, from the time he took to count it out. I imagine you have expenses, he said. She appreciated his understanding.

You are very generous, monsieur. So I'm told, Alston answered and closed the door, descending the stairs into what was left of the blue Paris night.

~

Now in the night around him the clouds were blowing across the sky, revealing a half moon, enough light for Pratt to see the steeple in the distant village. Then the shell whistled and the hillside behind Pratt blew apart. A direct hit on the gun position concealed by dirt and stumps. Pratt ran into the smoking debris.

The soldier's face was slippery with blood. Pratt put his ear to the man's mouth, trying to make sense of his sounds. The soldier moaned. His teeth chattered. Then his mouth opened. Blood poured out. His eyes rolled back in his head. The sounds stopped. Pratt arranged the man on the ground. He spread his fingers over the man's skin and felt warmth go out of the body.

"Three, sir. Three dead," a corporal reported.

"And Doyle here. Four," Pratt replied.

"I hope he at least got to enjoy his chocolate," the corporal said.

"What are you talking about?" Pratt asked.

"Doyle went into the village yesterday and bought chocolate at the café."

Pratt knew Doyle. He was from the Midwest and friendly. Only eighteen. Fond of talking to people.

The sky wasn't clear anymore. The German gunners took the rest of the night off.

"I'm going into the village," Pratt told Alston the next day.

Monsieur Devon was a thin man who walked with a limp. He was about thirty and said he'd received a wound early in the war. Before you Americans came, he added with sarcasm. He ran the café with his wife. They had a child, a little boy with brown eyes and a round face.

Devon always had wine and chocolate for sale, and oranges sometimes, besides cheese, bread, and meat.

"What are your pleasures?" he asked. He wiped the counter

with a folded cloth. Pratt leaned on the counter and stared at Devon, but the man kept wiping and would not look into Pratt's eyes.

"A bad business last night," Devon said.

"The guns, you mean?"

"Oui, monsieur, the German guns."

"They didn't hurt us much," Pratt said. "They were aiming at the wrong hill."

"Ah," Devon uttered. He refolded the cloth. "Would you care to sample some Sauterne? It's a local favorite. No charge."

"A glass for each of us," Pratt said.

Devon took down a clear bottle with yellowish wine inside and poured some into three glasses. Alston held his glass up to the light, then inhaled the sweet aroma.

"Victoire." The three touched glasses. "The wrong hill, you said?"

"We're on the other side. Half a kilometer away."

"You are lucky then. My wine brings you luck."

"We came to buy some more."

Pratt and Alston left the café with a bottle of red and some squares of dark chocolate wrapped in wax paper. Clouds kept the German planes on the ground, but in a few hours the 77s would start firing again.

When they did they targeted half a kilometer over the hill from where they had aimed the night before. The shells exploded into empty ammunition pits the French had left behind earlier in the war. Some abandoned shells for the French 75s exploded, giving the impression to the German lookouts that the attack was successful.

"Do you like this wine?"

"Not anymore," Pratt said.

Pratt gave the chocolate to one of the messengers, along with the note about Devon to take to the post east of the village.

The next day the overcast deepened, a good time for the Americans to move the artillery. By the end of the day the guns, the caissons, the ration wagons, the water wagons, and the rest of the men and equipment of the battery were on their way to a new position.

A few weeks later Pratt heard that the French had found a phone in Devon's house that he used to contact the Germans. He asked for mercy. The French executed him in the garden beside the café.

"I would have considered mercy," Pratt said.

"I wouldn't," Alston said.

~

The Germans were on the run now. By late September Pratt and Alston joined French and English troops near Verdun. A few days later both men were sick with the influenza. They recovered. In another month the war ended and both men went to Paris.

They encountered several Harvard people who hung around the Crillon. One evening Pratt and Alston were standing by themselves at the bar talking softly about staying in Paris or going home. Neither one noticed Annette. She had missed Alston and wanted to be with him. She was annoyed to find him passing time with Pratt.

"Have a good time with yourselves," she said when the men saw her reflection in the mirror behind the bar and turned around. She walked out of the room.

Alston remembered where she lived. If the mood struck him, he might find himself in her neighborhood, but not tonight. He wanted a nice dinner and some brandy afterward. He wanted to hear men laughing. He wanted to let his mind leave the war.

Pratt didn't want company. For a while he walked in the Place de la Concorde. Almost everywhere else was full of noise and all sorts of soldiers and civilians having a good time. Why not? he asked himself. He ended up at a music club near the Seine.

He leaned against the wall and listened to the band and watched people dancing. One of the musicians, the man who played the saxophone, was a Negro, and the singer, who sang in French, was colored too. Sometimes Pratt imagined his mother singing, imagined her in the cool summer mornings in the wash-house, light shining through the windows on her skin, her shadow crossing the chalky wall.

"Your people are very popular now."

The voice spoke behind him. Pratt recognized Annette's perfume.

"You have come to be with them?" She smiled, not a friendly smile at all. "They say the saxophone man has many skills, that it goes with his race."

Scanning Pratt's features, his smooth hair, his narrow nose and lips, skin no darker than hers, Annette wondered if Pratt had lied.

Pratt wanted to push her away but he stood there, bent over to make out her words in the air full of shrilling chords.

"Your friend, he knows how to do things. Such a shame about you," she said. She reached up and patted his cheek.

A man asked Annette to dance. When she disappeared into the crowd, Pratt left the club. The next day he was offered accommodation on a ship sailing to America. It was almost Christmas.

Alston found the company at the Crillon enjoyable and decided to stay on. Christmas in Paris appealed to him. Soon the Crillon would be buzzing with people working out the details of the peace treaty. It might be useful to his future career to stay around and fit in.

. . . Presley, you thought often about your father in those times we spent underground in the war. You checked your watch and remarked on what your father would be doing on his side of the Atlantic. Pouring himself a whiskey, you guessed, sitting down to read the papers. I had to invent the room, and I had not met Walter yet, but I had seen your father materializing from Leavitt & Pierce with a clutch of cigars and casting his eyes over Jimmy and me, so I could see your father too. We shared him, though I realize my saying so makes you shiver with disgust. You want nothing of yours to touch anything of mine. Annette, though, is another matter.

Tulliver, my father, never took up many of my own thoughts. When

I remembered home, I mostly thought of the river and its sulfur smell, the fields, the cotton, the horses, the gardens, the lizards scuttling across the palmetto leaves, the heat.

Presley, did your father ever say, I love you? Did he ever embrace you? My father didn't say those words to me. He hardly bothered with me at all. Mrs. Bennet and the Bennets' servants tended me until I went away to school. Of course my father had saved me, had gone to Charleston to rescue me from my mother's family. Surely Tulliver cared for me. He loved me in his way. Sometimes he would let me watch him paint. Wonder filled me as he brushed onto the canvas shapes and colors in front of us, changing them, bending them, deepening them. And of course it was the painting of my mother that haunted me, her skin, the contours of her neck, her shoulders, the light in the white room glowing on her skin, on her back. For hours I hunkered by the gardenias watching my father paint. He had long, thin arms. I could see the muscle under his skin flexing and unflexing. He always wore a thick bracelet on his right wrist, silver set with turquoises, a gift from an admirer. Once he had been a man who spent much of his time with women. He was like you in that way. But if he had been loved by a woman as generous and lovely as Mina, he never would have treated her the way you treated Mina. I suppose you think she deserved it, though.

We're alike too, you and I, Presley. We hid our lives from our fathers. Perhaps yours found out about Mina, but not when it made any difference. My father never found out about my attempt to find my mother's grave. He never knew I lost my toe. I told the headmaster I'd been attacked by some men who stole my camera. The Headmaster suggested on my next visit home I tell my father the truth. I didn't. It would have vexed Tulliver, my interest in my mother. I would no more have told him than I would have asked him if he had loved my mother or if she had loved him.

My father never knew about Mr. Purdy either, nor any of the things the detective your father hired found out about me. It must have been a shock to you to find out I was alive.

~ ~ ~

"What do you see?"

For a moment Lieutenant Philip Lanier Pratt wondered what his father meant, for it had been his father years before who had stood beside Philip sharing a mirror and told him he was white. Such a fact was not a rejection of Philip's mother or her people, but an obvious conclusion given that the features of his father dominated those of his mother, not to mention the unfortunate truth that she had died after being disinherited by her people so that none of her family cared a whit about Philip, had forgotten him completely. Tulliver Pratt had sheltered and provided for his son at much expense as well as some philosophical embarrassment to himself. He believed in self-control and considered a carnal nature something he had left behind after he had sown his wild oats years earlier in Savannah and New Orleans.

Philip saw in his own sense of life as a young man no reason to disregard Tulliver's logic. Now for an instant Philip wondered if his father had changed his mind, or if some revealing feature had appeared not present before. Sometimes Philip dreamed his white skin turned soggy and fell apart, like newspapers in the rain, revealing his dark skin underneath.

Tulliver said, "I meant to call attention to your hair. It's beginning to show a bit of gray. Mine did that when I was about your age."

Tulliver was smoking one of the small Tampa cigars he favored. The two were watching from the window. The January sun had melted the frost. In the distance the horses that Philip remembered so fondly in France, or ones like them, were making their way from the barn toward the bare willows by the river.

The land belonged to the Bennets. Cotton land. During the war the government bought a lot of cotton. The owners of the plantations along the Santee prospered. Mr. Bennet had come to

South Carolina from New Britain, Connecticut, where his family owned a tool business, which Mr. Bennet was deemed too unreliable to take charge of. He borrowed money from his father to buy the Carolina land and the smaller version of the original house– called Palmetto and long since destroyed by fire– from an owner about his own age who was genuinely irresponsible, whereas Mr. Bennet turned out to have good sense and to be a hard worker.

Mr. Bennet married, then fathered a daughter. One summer afternoon Tulliver Pratt had appeared with a sketchbook and asked permission to draw what was left of the original Palmetto, which was the ocher-brick summer kitchen and some foundation stones, once ship's ballast, as well as the fountain in the azalea garden, copper naiads clasping hands around a phallic ornament meant to propel water into the air but now merely protruding and thickening its green patina year after year. Discovering that Tulliver had a knowledge of Latin, music, poetry, and some history, Mr. Bennet hired him to be his daughter's tutor. He judged the boys in the local county school, those whose parents either considered them unworthy of private education or could not afford it, unacceptable schoolmates for his daughter. Another school, of sorts, existed too, the one colored children attended on an irregular basis, referred to as the Jeepers.

Tulliver had never sat Philip down and chronicled the events Philip should consider to be the essence of his immediate family history. Tulliver would instead refer to events, saying, When I was doing such and such I met so and so or did this and that. Through references Philip knew that Tulliver had taken an interest in sketching children and had frequently gone to the Jeepers, where he sat quietly on a stool in the corner of the wooden, one-room building and drew the faces that appealed to him. He also knew that Tulliver sketched some of the black women who worked on different plantations, ones he saw at the grocery store or making their way up the road on Sunday to church. One of these women worked on the Perry plantation nearby. Her name was Ella.

Philip's mother. I drew your momma on Sunday afternoons, Tulliver recollected.

More than sketches. He used those to create the oil painting that Mr. Bennet deemed worthy to be hung on his wall beside others he and his wife had acquired, works mostly French, full of bright rooms where ladies practiced dancing or streets where people strolled or sat at tables in the shade of umbrellas. Philip's mother reclined on a bed in a room with white walls, her caramel skin radiant and smooth, the swelling of her hips displayed toward the viewer, her face turned away. " I can almost smell her" was the comment uttered in erotic approval by more than one guest who lingered before the collection. Tulliver at his best, Mr. Bennet remarked.

What interested Philip was his mother's pose, her face turned away. She had been turned away from him, not intentionally but by sickness. Within a year of his birth, she had died of scarlet fever. She had returned to her family in Charleston to have Philip. There Tulliver rescued Philip after she died. Her family wanted nothing to do with the child, the light-skinned son of a white man who rejected the family's request for money to provide for the child's survival.

One time Philip set out to find his mother's grave. He was sixteen then. Mr. Bennet advanced Tulliver money to pay Philip's tuition at Wheeler, a small academy in Charleston that both men expected to prepare Philip to pass the requirements to enter college up North. Philip left the grounds near Market Street and made his way to the part of the city that fit Tulliver's description of where his mother's family lived and where she was buried, he believed, in one of the old pieces of unwanted ground once set apart for slaves.

Philip had borrowed a Kodak to take a picture of the grave. He had difficulty finding the cemetery. Twilight streaked the sky. Laughter and the smell of cooking filled the air. "What you here for?" the man asked, a long, lanky man in overalls with ribbons in his hair. The men with him leaned closer to hear what Philip was going to say, each grinning as if it didn't matter what he said or who he was. They would have his camera.

Philip explained that he was looking for the cemetery where his mother was buried. Suddenly it did matter what he said and who he was. "Ain't nobody but us buried here," the man said. "Your momma be here, then you ain't white like you look. You like us."

One of the men pulled the camera out of Philip's hand. Another opened a knife and deftly cut off the top button of Philip's shirt. The lanky man ripped the shirt open.

"You sure do look white," the lanky man said. The others hummed their agreement. "I bet you forget you ain't." The others nodded. "We need to give you a way so you remember."

They dragged Philip off the dirt street into overgrown weeds and threw him on ground that smelled like piss. "Undo your boot, boy." Philip unlaced it. One of the men yanked it off, and the sock.

"Catch a nigger by the toe. You heard that, boy? Since you don't want to be no nigger, you don't need all them toes. We need a spare in case your white daddy wants to catch one of us."

The others laughed. Then two grabbed Philip, pinned him in the weeds, pressed hands over his mouth. The man with the knife bore down and cut into the bone of Philip's little toe. Philip vomited and lost consciousness. Then pain woke him. The men were gone. It was dark. Dizzy with pain, Philip crawled through the weeds to the street. A woman leaning over one of the balconies of a narrow wooden house saw him. She saw the blood and raised him up. Mr. Purdy will help you, she said. Philip held onto her as she led him along the street and to a corner room of a house damp and decaying. She tapped on the door. A man in a white coat opened it.

Philip lay back on a leather cushion. Mr. Purdy washed the wound and stopped the bleeding. He crossed some strips of bandage loosely over Philip's foot. Mr. Purdy parted his thick gray hair on the side. Deep wrinkles surrounded his eyes. He wore a shirt with a buttoned collar and no tie. The coat smelled of carbolic. Philip explained who he was searching for.

"You must be an Etoy," he said when Philip told him about his mother. "They had light skin. She more than the rest, but them too. It takes more than one generation to get skin like hers."

"Are you a doctor?" Philip asked.

"Oh no. Though I had training. I'm a mechanic. I fix broke things, people mostly. Do what much I can."

"Mr. Purdy's as good as any doctor," the woman said.

"The truth, however, is I am not a doctor and you need one, young man. I'll take you. I have a Ford."

Mr. Purdy cranked the car, then drove Philip toward the lights of Market Street. The hospital was near Philip's school.

"I didn't know my momma," Philip said.

"I knew her a little." Mr. Purdy smiled. "The other light-skinned ones moved away or got sick and died young like your momma. The only ones left here are the dark ones. They curse the ones with what they call the good skin, but they envy them too. My advice is, don't come back here. Next time you might lose more than your little toe and your Kodak."

When Mr. Purdy left Philip at the hospital, he said, "You know, you should have lied, just told those men who stopped you that you were there for some carnal adventure. They'd understand and probably send you where you needed to go. It's a sad thing, but I've found that people, white and black, will tolerate a carnal relationship between races. It's love they won't accept."

Home from France for several weeks, Philip did little more than ride Mr. Bennet's horses and try to free his mind of the war. The few friends he had previously made were schoolmates who lived in Charleston, but he had no wish to renew those connections. Philip preferred solitude. He did not make friends easily. In this way he was like his father.

Philip had one friend, Presley Medford Alston.

. . . I missed you, Presley. I did not want to deceive you. I thought you would understand. I thought Annette would understand too. She was the first person I ever told about my mother.

I had been walking along a row of lindens when Annette appeared. She smiled and told me she could take me to some cabarets I'd like. Maybe we could go to her room later on. I didn't intend to go home with her and I wouldn't have, but we ran into Captain Connors and I introduced him to Annette. He wouldn't touch her hand. No one would touch my hand either if they could see what I was. I had a white skin and a black skin too. I felt sorry for her.

She was very patient. She guided my hands over her breasts and told me how endowed I was. I began to think about the painting of my mother. The painted lady. I hid my smile from Annette. I wasn't interested in Annette, whom I could reach out and touch. I was interested in the woman I could never touch, the woman with her back turned to me.

I needed to tell someone about her. To tell someone was to make her real. I needed to invent the face I could not see.

I did not respond to Annette. She was displeased. Petulant. How did you lose your toe? she asked, implying a toe wasn't the only thing missing about me. I told her. At first she didn't understand why the men would stop me and do such a thing. Then I could see her figuring it out. She leaned forward and held the sheet against her breasts. You are a Negro? she asked. Before I answered she was already sliding out of bed. She disappeared behind the screen where she had left her clothes.

Of course I had not seen Annette again until we were at the bar at the Crillon after the war. It never crossed my mind you knew her too. I wanted to tell you what I had told her in case you and Annette met again. I tried. I wrote several letters in my head. I couldn't. I was afraid. It's one thing to tell a person in another country you think you'll never see again, quite a different thing to tell your friend. How relieved I was you wrote me. You invited me to your parents' house at the end of August. You said the women you met in Paris were liber-

ated and fun to be with and asked me if I remembered the woman who had spoken to us at the bar. What was her name? you asked. Annette, wasn't it? Paris is a big city. You'd never seen her again, you said; but if you ever did, you would tell her how rude she had been.

When I looked in the mirror, a white man looked back. But not a man as white as you.

~ ~ ~

From his position at the bar in the Crillon, Presley observed the famous and the obscure, the *haut monde* and the *demi-monde*. Annette reappeared one evening with Johns, a lord with one arm, the other lost at the Somme. He invited Presley to join their table. I seem to attract men with missing parts, Annette said after Johns excused himself to consult with another member of the English delegation seated nearby. Presley looked down at his shoe and recalled Annette mentioning an American who was missing a toe. Not until this minute did he connect the man in Annette's story with Philip Pratt.

"Take me swimming," Annette said.

"When?"

"Tomorrow. Let's make it a holiday."

The next day they rode the train east toward Château-Thierry and took a room at Charly, a village where Annette said her cousins lived. Presley wondered if she intended to show him off. They rented a boat and rowed on the Marne, to a narrow place in the river where Annette swam before the war.

Presley undid the buttons between her breasts. The water flowed over the swimmers. Presley stroked lazily against the current. What he saw in the reeds along the bank reminded him of the bleached deer bones he found in the forest one summer in Vermont. He paddled closer for a look.

Nestled in the mud of the shore the connection of bones appeared, pale and clean, one tibia and femur, the harp of the chest stained brown, the skull submerged, distorted into shimmering curves beneath the sunny surface of the water. What army the bones had followed no longer obvious or relevant.

"*Dieu*, you are the only whole man I know," Annette said that night in bed.

"What about Philip, my friend?" Presley asked.

"The man without a toe? I told you about him. Remember?"

"Tell me more."

Annette repeated what Philip had told her.

~

August. The time neared for Philip to go North. He told himself to try again, to look for his mother's grave once more, the physical place where, perhaps, her spirit lingered, some incorporeal part of her that might communicate with him, might answer his questions: Who are you? Did you love me? Maybe it was that spirit who nagged him, warning him he might never be in Charleston again.

He said good-bye to his father and drove away with Mr. Bennet, who had an errand to attend to in Charleston. There Philip would board the train to Washington, changing later to another for Boston. Mr. Bennet let Philip out in front of the white arches of the station amid the bustle of porters and passengers. Philip checked his suitcase at the luggage room and hired a taxi to Line Street, where Mr. Purdy had told him he would find the graveyard.

In the slant of the afternoon sun the small headstones leaned out of hard ground. Here and three a live oak offered a little shade, the roots thickening in clusters above the sparse, twiney grass. Some faded stems drooped from the flowers cups. Many of the stones, cracked into small pieces, lay flat on the ground. These had no names or decorations.

Etoy. Philip found the place. One stone, a bit whiter than the others. An obelisk, professionally prepared, the image of praying hands, the words "The family Etoy lieth here." Four dates and four names of Etoy followed, but Ella's not among them. Yet the shape of the ground suggested space for more than four burials. Raising the grass with the toe of his shoe, Philip found five small fieldstones, each to mark the location of a body, but which marked Ella's grave and not one of the named Philip would never know. He felt no spirits and no communication. Without taking a picture, he turned around and returned to the taxi, whose driver had nervously waited to convey Philip to the station.

In a few minutes Philip realized the car had turned onto the street where Mr. Purdy lived. There was the tangle of weeds. There was the house. "Wait," Philip said. "Wait. I want to visit someone."

The driver had already passed the house. He stopped the car. Philip walked back. On the side of the building the door was ajar. Philip heard an angry voice.

"You ain't no doctor. You pay me what you been paying or I'll turn you in."

"I can't pay you any more."

Philip recognized Mr. Purdy's voice.

Philip nudged the door. It opened enough for Philip to see the back of a man in a policeman's uniform and Mr. Purdy. The man held a nightstick in his hand. He lifted it up.

"I lay this beside your skull and you won't have a brain left in that fuzzy head of yours."

The man swung the stick, striking Mr. Purdy's chest hard enough to knock him backward.

"Do what you have to, but I can't pay."

The man raised the stick again. Philip pushed through the door. He grabbed what he saw, the shiny handle of the surgical knife on the tabletop. The policeman whirled around and Philip lunged. He was aiming for the shoulder but stuck the blade through the man's blue collar into the cartilage of his throat. The policeman made a stricken sound. His blood darkened the fabric. His breath fizzed out his mouth in little pink bubbles that burst on his lips. The stick fell from of his hand. His knees bent, slumping his body down, inch by inch, until the unbalanced weight dropped him to the floor. Dead weight, Philip thought. The man was going to bleed to death on the floor.

"I came . . ."

"Don't tell me now," Mr. Purdy said. He thrust a towel into Philip's hand. Philip wiped off the blood, cleaned the handle, and bundled the knife in the towel.

"Leave it. I'll attend to things. Leave everything. Leave now. "

Philip backed out the door. The driver was standing with his foot on the running board, his eyes delighting in the woman leaning from a window.

"Some other time," the driver hollered up.

"You think he's prettier than me?" the woman called as Philip was climbing into the car.

"Gotta work to afford you, don't I?" the driver answered, waving as he drove way. Another policeman stood in a doorway. He glanced at the car. Philip hunched down in the backseat.

In the whites' rest room at the station Philip took off his jacket and washed his face and hands. He tried to dry his shirt where sweat made it stick to his sides. Finally he put on his jacket, combed his hair, and collected his suitcase. He could still feel his heart beating. On the train he found his seat. After the train left the station, Philip washed his face and hands again. He sat down in one of the chairs by the door of the car. Tobacco juice streaked the linoleum around the spittoons. The man in the next chair folded his newspaper and took a flask from his pocket. He offered Philip a drink. The man's hair smelled of Fitch's tonic.

"Better have one, young man. The government's only giving us the rest of the year."

Philip swallowed and handed the man his flask.

"This Prohibition thing is all a bunch of damn nonsense cooked up by women with nothing better to do except agitate for the vote."

Philip scarcely heard what the man was saying, but he nodded his head anyway.

"You look like a man who almost missed his train. You must have run for it."

"I guess I did."

The man took a drink and lit a Sweet Caporal. "We win the war, now it's all these damn riots and strikes. One thing I tell you, niggers ought to be thankful for what we give 'em and not be causing trouble."

"I appreciated your whiskey, sir." Philip stood up and returned to his seat.

. . . You would have disliked him too, Presley, for another reason. He was ordinary. No better or no worse than anyone else, any other white man traveling on that train. I was a white man traveling on that train, or appeared to be.

My thoughts, as much as I could concentrate, were about Mr. Purdy. I had expected him to welcome me, enjoy seeing me again, because a part of my heritage was his. He more than Tulliver knew who I was. I felt his kindness toward me. In fact I had imagined that in his room I could be myself, a man of two races, of two worlds. So much arrogance, of course. I had to suffer what he had suffered to share his identity. I merely sympathized with his condition, only sorrowed for the way he lived his daily life. My anger toward the man who threatened Mr. Purdy was the reaction of a passerby, a visitor who encounters unfairness but has not lived it. If I had endured what he had endured, I would have ridden the train north feeling accomplishment, righteousness. I had attacked the attacker. Instead I needed to keep assuring myself he deserved what I had done. Although the man who offered me whiskey offended me, I did not tell him why. I was what I appeared to be, a white man traveling on the train. A man who was afraid. I could see blood and smell blood. I had committed a crime.

I remember on the ship when you came back from what you referred to as your obligation. You seemed to put it out of mind. The boat was pitching and swaying, and no one had confidence that he could kill the German with a rifle shot. So we formed a half circle on the stern, the German, too resolute to need support, in the middle, and you raised the revolver to the man's head at the place and angle the doctor instructed you, and fired. That was the first time I smelled blood. I believe many of us closed our eyes before you shot. I know I did.

∾ ∾ ∾

The sun glowed overhead and warmed him. Adele Alston, Presley's mother, disapproved of his removing his shirt when he sailed. The midday heat blotched the skin, she warned; but he took off his shirt anyway.

Presley brought the boat about and tacked across the bay. Lily, his sister, would be watching through the telescope mounted on the tripod in the balcony window of the library on the second floor. She was always spying on people. When she was younger she turned the most innocent peepings, as she called them– family picnics on the rocks, servants hanging out laundry, her mother's friends taking tea on the terrace– into elaborate stories of spies and dangerous attractions. Lily, where do you get such awful ideas? their mother asked. Presley had wondered the same thing. Perhaps Lily elaborated the shared gossip of her classmates at Miss Prentice's School, but those young ladies belonged to homes where children were unlikely to hear about harems, white slavery, the opium trade, or even the more mundane transactions of the flesh in Scollay Square.

At the dinner table in the Boston house, after his return from France, Presley was aware of silences, not that the conversation was always lively and uninterrupted in the past, moments when he sensed Lily and his parents regarding him, taking his measure, determining the ways the war had changed him. In the halls, too, the servants discreetely eyed Presley with interest, particularly Mary, who did the laundry and helped in the kitchen. The sun on Presley's skin and the thought of Mary's white, ample breasts aroused him. Best not let it happen tomorrow when he was with his father's guests, the men all naked, parading from the boathouse to the salty, wrinkled waters of the bay that smelled sweet and bitter like the private parts of a woman. He wondered if Mary, collecting his linen from the hamper, had discovered his smell and ever thought about him as he did her.

Presley came about again and headed downwind toward the house, called the "cottage," a rambling wood-and-shingle structure of many rooms wrapped by porches decorated with elaborate adornments of wood. One day the cottage would belong to him, it and the Boston home on Louisburg Square. Lily would inherit their grandmother's money, Presley the property and their father's money. Year after year Lily and their father grew more distant from each other, more aloof.

What do you want to do with yourself? his father had asked after Presley's second year at Harvard. I imagine something in government service, diplomatic work, Presley replied. But on this last day of August 1919, he was thinking about football. Practice began in two days. He wondered what sort of shape he'd be in. Perhaps he should have gone to the gym in Paris where some of the Americans lobbed medicine balls to each other or boxed. Pratt was probably doing wind sprints.

~

"The Hendersons and the Bridgers will be staying over," Adele said.

Everet Alston raised his eyes from the previous day's *Evening Transcript*. Adele walked across the room to the window. She lifted the edge of the curtain. Light widened down the room.

"See anything?"

"Presley sailing."

"Use the telescope. Have a better look. Lily was watching a minute ago."

"I'd rather not."
"Rather not what?"
"Don't be so irritable. You know what I mean."
"I don't think I'm as difficult as you've been lately."
"With Presley coming home, and the party, I've had too much to do. I apologize for being difficult."
"I think we're both having a hard time adjusting to Presley."
"I wish he'd share some of his experiences with us."
"How much do you really want to know?"
Adele let go of the curtain. The room darkened. "You're right, Everet. I don't want to know much. Certainly not the details of his soldier's life. I'm his mother but he's not my child anymore."
"He understands duty and loyalty. I'm very proud of him," Mr. Alston said thinking of Arthur, his brother, the family disgrace, who didn't understand loyalty and duty at all.
"You've always understood them well too, Everet."
"I hope you're not condemning that."
"Of course not."
"What about his friend? Pratt. Did he answer your invitation to stay with us?"
"Lieutenant Pratt wrote he would be most pleased to accept our invitation."
"He does have some manners then."
"But you disapprove."
"I've always encouraged Presley to be democratic in choosing his friends. I don't want him to know only the Gold Coast crowd. Mr. Pratt was a fine end on the football team and I'm sure an admirable officer as well."
"What don't you like about him?"
The word traitor came to Mr. Alston's mind. Philip's essay defending a German, which Presley had told him about, was something Mr. Alston could not dismiss as quickly as did Presley. He had even suggested it took courage to write such a piece.
"He wrote an essay defending the Harvard professor who was

spreading the Kaiser's propaganda to the students."

"I thought Mr. Lowell defended him too."

"Mr. Lowell is the president. Mr. Pratt was a freshman on a scholarship who required a year of tutoring before he could pass the entrance examinations. In any case I think he needs Presley more than Presley needs him."

"Who are you talking about?" Lily interrupted.

Lily stood in the doorway. "One of your brother's friends, Lily. Someone you'll meet tomorrow," Mrs. Alston said. The expression on Mr. Alston's face warned his wife to say nothing more.

Tomorrow was very much on Lily's mind. She had considered her plan carefully, such a dangerous plan she couldn't tell it even to Esther, her best friend. The guests would all be in the house by noon. The bed of coals and flavoring wood would be set alight. Drinks would be offered. At one o'clock, or near about, her father would invite the men to withdraw with him to the boathouse. She wasn't sure how long it took men to undress. When they had done that, they would follow her father out of the boathouse and down the rocks that concealed the men from anyone watching from the windows in the house. She knew the flat place they dove from and the shelved face of rock where they climbed up from the sea, shivering. At least she imagined them shivering. She had never dared sneak close enough to peep.

At supper that night Lily asked who else was coming tomorrow. The usual crowd, her mother said. Not much excitement there. Lily had seen her father naked. Her brother also. Better, but one could think of one's brother only in general terms. She had looked quickly and turned away. Senator Bridgers and Judge Henderson were about her father's age, and just as saggy and uninteresting. However, the Hoffsetters had twin sons who were starting Dartmouth in a few days. They were friends of the Wulfurts' son who would be going back to Yale. He had been gassed in the war and could speak only in a whisper. Then there was Pres's friend, Pratt, the one from the South. Of course she'd listened at the door and heard what her father had said. She'd heard her father speak about him before too. Her father didn't care for people from the South.

Philip sat staring out the train window. Far ahead, in another world almost, the locomotive hooted. Puffs of smoke dissolved in the gray, late-summer air. The leaves on the maples were already deepening to red. Here and there he saw houses and factories in the distance. Minutes later he could almost reach out and touch the wash drying on the clotheslines in tiny backyards. He was carried forward but he didn't seem to move from where he had been.

Philip had eaten a sandwich. When was that? When had he slept? The train slowed through the necklace of cities between New York and Connecticut and sped past Saybrook, where the track ran so close to the ocean it appeared to touch the foamy sprawl of tide; roared over the iron bridge above the Thames at New London; then wove through Rhode Island and into Massachusetts.

Philip knew he was going to be late. He did not want to disappoint Presley or inconvenience his family, yet he had a difficult time concentrating on time present or future, especially the Alstons' invitation. The immediate past, much as he tried to push it out of his mind, wouldn't leave. Could Mr. Purdy do what he said, take care of things, make everything all right again? Philip saw himself wiping the policeman's blood off his hands.

"I think everyone's here but your friend," Adele said. Scanning the faces in the room, she didn't see Lily's, but Lily had been there just a few moments earlier. The announcement didn't concern Lily anyway.

"Perhaps he's not coming after all," Mr. Alston added.

"He'll be here," Presley assured them.

Walter, the servant who had passed the tray of drinks, handed

Mr. Alston a tiny silver bell. Mr. Alston flicked his wrist like a doctor shaking down mercury in a thermometer. The bell tinkled.

"We gather to celebrate the end of summer and the bounty summer has generously given us. The lobsters and mussels are warming nicely, the potatoes and corn will soon be tender, so I invite any man to follow me who cares to invigorate his appetite. Please bring your refreshments with you."

As soon as the men left, the ladies returned to their conversations. Adele looked around again for her daughter. "Walter, have you seen Lily?"

"Miss Lily felt cold and went to her room to dress in something warmer."

"Thank you, Walter," Adele said, and turned her attention to Judge Henderson's wife, who was repeating that her husband feared a police strike in Boston.

"Unheard of. Police on strike. Simply unheard of," Mrs. Bridgers lamented.

~

Lily had taken off her dress and put on a pair of tennis trousers and a cardigan. Unobserved, she had gone out of the cottage and climbed up the ladder in the boathouse to the beams overhead, then slipped down into one of the shells her father used to row on the lake in Vermont.

She heard the men on the path. She recognized Judge Henderson's voice calling out to her father, asking the longest time anyone had spent in the water. About two minutes, her father answered. Must have been shriveled to a nub, the Judge said. The others laughed. The door creaked wider. Lily took a deep breath and pressed against the bottom of the shell.

~

"A car has arrived," Walter informed Mrs. Alston.

"Oh?"

"A young man."

"Probably Lieutenant Pratt. Did he give you his card?"

"No, ma'am."

"I'll see to him. Pass more drinks."

Adele found Philip, dressed in linen trousers and jacket, standing by the front door, his leather case beside him.

"Lieutenant Pratt, I'm Adele Alston, Presley's mother. We're glad you've arrived."

"I apologize that I'm late." He started to pick up his case.

"Leave your luggage. One of the help will take it to your room. Presley and the others have gone to the boathouse for a swim. Hurry along, then, or you'll miss out." From the door Mrs. Alston indicated the way Philip should go. She was aware of addressing him as a servant or a child, perhaps because he had only one small bag and owned, she assumed, no more than a servant or a child would own.

~

Lily had not dared to raise herself enough to see over the edge of the shell and observe the men below. Every time she moved, the shell tipped, and she clung to keep from falling out. Not the entrance she had in mind, crashing at the feet of naked men like some gawky bird shot in flight. The men were gone now. Their clothes folded on the chairs behind a curtain hung in loops from wire attached to the beams to create privacy. From her hiding place Lily could see into nearly every one of the tiny dressing spaces. Directly under her she saw the Judge's garters, dark blue trousers, and maroon suspenders. The Judge never wore seersucker or linen to the seacoast, always wool. Keeps out the heat, he believed.

Under the roof, the hot air hung full of the spicy smells of resin and varnish. Sweat dampened the curls along the side of Lily's head. Carefully she edged her way out of the shell, crossed the beam, and climbed down the ladder. Then she heard new footsteps. She dipped behind the row of oars and paddles leaning against the wall on the other side of the room opposite the curtain. Peering out, she saw Philip. He had taken off his jacket and tie and was looking for an empty place to undress. He laid his jacket on the table where some of the others had left their refreshment glasses. He slipped his suspenders from his shoulders, unbuttoned his shirt and put it on the table too, slipped off his shoes, removed his trousers, adding them to the pile, then his undershirt, and, turning sideways, his socks and undershorts.

He stood naked. He picked up one of the glasses and tipped it to his lips. Lily tried to hold her breath. The dust and dampness tingled her nose. She pressed her palm against her face, but not over her eyes. Lower and lower she studied this man, this Lieutenant Pratt her father doesn't care for, this lovely form, who picks up a towel from the stack near the curtain and wraps it around his waist before he disappears out the door.

Lily stepped between a pair of oars and ran out the other door and up the path to the house. She closed the kitchen screen behind her. Walter was uncorking bottles of wine.

"Been peeping again, Miss Lily?"

She shook her head. Walter smiled. "Of course you haven't."

~

Presley waved to Philip. Everyone had dried off and now sat on the rocks facing the sun. How healthy they felt when they were out of the numbing water and could take a deep breath again. Their skin tingled. This was the time Mr. Alston enjoyed most. Men washed by the ancient sea sitting together in peace, sharing moments with the younger generation. No women to defer to. One could speak one's mind. But no one was speaking now. All watched the newcomer. He strode to the water's edge, dove in, and swam underwater away from land until he surfaced, then stroked toward land again with a smooth crawl.

"More than two minutes, I'd guess. Quite impressive," the Judge remarked. The Hoffsetter twins nodded agreement.

Showing off, Mr. Alston thought. Young Wulfurt watched with pale empty eyes as the newcomer climbed out of the water and took the towel Presley handed him.

~

Tables had been carried to the lawn. The sun sparkled on glass bowls and silver pitchers, gleamed on the jewelry the ladies wore and the place settings arranged on the linen. The guests were served from platters of clams, mussels, lobsters, corn on the cob, and potatoes, all cooked over coals, steamed in the vapors of apple branches and seaweed. Lily, who had changed her clothes again and now wore a white crepe dress chosen because she thought it improved her figure, was seated between the Hoffsetter twins across from Philip. Mr. Alston sat at the head of the table, Presley on his left and Mrs. Henderson on his right.

"Presley, tell us about Paris," Mrs. Henderson said.

"I can tell you I had a good time," he answered.

"I'm sure you deserved it," she replied.

"Tell us something you did in the war," one of the twins said.

Mr. Alston put down his butter knife. Lily, too, looked at her brother. Despite their questions, he had told them practically nothing of his experiences.

"In the field artillery you shoot your gun but you don't really see what you hit," Presley said.

The twin sat waiting for more.

"My brother means he hasn't any tales of clanging sabers and spilling blood. That's just heroic rot anyway," Lily interrupted.

Mrs. Henderson blinked in surprise. Presley reddened with anger. "Lily gets carried away with her words," Mr. Alston said. "Quite a vivid imagination," he noted, a criticism more than a defense.

"Tell them about the man on the boat," Philip said.

Again Mr. Alston and Lily eyed Presley.

"Crossing the Atlantic we were under orders not to make noise or show lights in case a German ship might spot us. The third night all the lights came on for about a minute, then went off. Next night, same thing. Nothing for a couple of nights after that. Then lights again. Turned out one of the cooks was a German."

"Pres found him at the switches."

"What happened to him?" the other twin asked.

"He was punished," Presley answered.

"How was he punished?" Mr. Alston asked in a quiet voice that his wife and the Judge, seated at the other end of the table, couldn't hear.

"He was shot," Presley answered.

"Oh my," Mrs. Henderson exclaimed.

"I suppose it had to be done" said Mr. Alston.

"Who shot him?" a twin asked.

"I did," Presley said.

"My goodness." Mrs. Henderson patted her cheek with her napkin.

Lily was staring at Presley with her mouth open. When she looked away, she found Philip staring at her.

"Let's talk about something else," Mr. Alston said. But after the guests had risen from the table and stood in small groups on the lawn sipping the warm muscat Mr. Alston was fond of, he took the Judge aside and impressed him with what Presley had done.

"No nonsense about that boy. You've got a winner there," the Judge said.

Lily found Philip by himself. "Did you do anything brave like my brother did?" she asked. Philip hadn't known Lily long enough to detect the irony.

"Of course."

"Tell me."

"I used to carry a full cup of coffee from the food wagon to the dugout during an air raid and never spill a drop."

"I'm almost eighteen. You don't have to treat me like a child."

"I apologize," Philip said. "I thought you'd understand."

Lily pressed her bottom teeth into her lip the way she did when she was concentrating. "What Presley did wasn't brave, you're saying?" She agreed with that. Shooting a captive might be necessary but it wasn't heroic or brave.

"I'm saying it was brave to go about one's business, shells blowing holes all around you. We all did it."

Lily smiled. "The French women, they all kissed you for your bravery?"

"A few did."

"A few? I bet dozens. Hundreds."

"A few."

Lily stood very close to Philip. "Would you like me to kiss you?" she asked.

Philip laughed. Not the reaction she'd expected.

"I'm very flattered," he said.

"And I will sometime. You know I will," Lily replied. While her eyes held his attention, she reached out, took the glass of wine from his hand, gulped it down, pushed the glass into his hand again, and walked away.

~

Evening spread over the sea. Philip and Presley changed clothes. They found a football and threw it back and forth and tucked it under their arms and sprinted across the grass until they bent over laughing.

Later that night, Lily found a half-full bottle of champagne and crept outside. She drank it watching the house, watching the lights go out one by one. The more she drank, the clearer she remembered Philip's body. She touched her own, glided the tip of her tongue back and forth on her lips pretending her mouth was his.

TWO

. . . I couldn't sleep. After you went to bed, I stood outside and watched Lily. She seemed as alone as I was. She acted older, more confident, than I. I was in awe of her. If I had never met her again, I would never have forgotten her. I watched her sitting by herself drinking wine. I was attracted to her, and if she had been older I would have sat beside her and shared the wine. We would have ended up kissing. I warned myself not to betray you, our friendship, kissing Lily. She was too young. But you, whose reputation for lovemaking wasn't secret, considered her younger than she was, fifteen instead of seventeen, as if you wanted to protect her from men such as yourself who might take advantage of her.

I made myself think of football. Coach Haughton had resigned and Fisher was taking his place. With you and me and Phinney and the others returning from the war, we had the making of a good team. You talked a lot about an undefeated season. You convinced me we could have one. Our team would forever be special, be remembered. Our pictures would look out of the trophy cases in the lobby of the gym, beside the game balls inked with the scores. Your excitement was contagious. I could feel it despite the fact that I could not forget what had happened in Charleston. College was sanctuary. I could hide in its rooms. I could put on my uniform and no one would recognize me.

I hadn't counted on all the photographers meeting the team. Each click of a shutter put me on edge. They posed you passing and running. Show us your famous straight-arm, they said. You obliged until Fisher said it was time to go to work.

~ ~ ~

"Gentlemen, we have work to do," Fisher said to the reporters, who had been interviewing the seven players returning from the war.

The rest of the squad was clambering out of the locker room now. A hundred men, their cleats grinding the cinders. The squad would do some stretching and calisthenics today. Tomorrow would be harder.

Coach Fisher, who had started on the 1912 squad, stood shorter than Presley. Fisher took off his cap and brushed his hand over his hair. The sun flashed on the golden rims of his eyeglasses.

"Mr. Alston, lead the way," Fisher said.

Philip fell into a jog behind Presley, with Phinney, the other end, running beside him. Philip could hear Clark behind them grumbling about his stiff legs. He weighed over two hundred pounds and played guard.

"You and Pres rooming together, I heard."

"In Mower," Philip answered.

Presley stopped in the middle of the practice field. The others circled around him. One of the assistants called out the exercise. Jumping jacks first. Presley jumped back and forth, raising and lowering his arms, slapping his palms against the sides of his pants. The rest of the squad did the same thing. By the time they were doing push-ups, Philip could hear Clark breathing hard, cursing the humid air.

Coach Fisher and Pooch Donovan, the trainer, wandered among the players, watching but not saying much. Donovan stood over Philip finishing his stretches. "Legs feel all right?"

"I did some running this summer," Philip answered.

"Good, because tomorrow we'll see if you're still the fastest man on the team."

The players returned to the locker room, showered, and changed clothes. Philip had walked to the stadium from the Yard and expected to walk back again. A few cars were parked outside the stadium.

"Want a ride?" Presley asked. He took out his handkerchief and brushed specks of dust off the dark green fender. The roadster's top was folded down and Philip smelled the scent of new leather .

They drove over the bridge and up Boylston, then Presley turned right onto Mt. Auburn and parked the Stutz at the curb near the entrance to the Hounds. White paint gleamed on the columns surrounding the wide front door and on the shutters opened to windows now golden with light.

Presley shut off the motor. "I'm going use the club's telephone. See you at dinner," he said.

Philip walked up Holyoke Street toward the Square. He waited to let a yellow streetcar go by and glimpsed the face of a girl staring out, then crossed Massachusetts Avenue and walked toward the Common before he went through the gates into Harvard Yard between Massachusetts Hall and Harvard Hall. He stopped. A hush filled the air, a memorial silence, deep and abiding. Washington had drilled his troops on the ground where Philip stood. The soldiers had slept in these plain buildings whose bricks glowed red in the ending day.

On the other side of the street, outside the Yard, several of the General's men moldered in the Old Burying Ground beside the Unitarian church. The dry leaves of the oaks and elms fluttered in the air. Philip thought of the tiny flags on the soldiers' graves he'd seen from the train window going from Paris to Le Havre on his way home.

Serene the Yard, quiet before it filled with students. Here and there lights flickered on in the rooms of faculty and tutors. Mr. Purdy's room was far, far away.

Philip walked past Hollis and saw a light in Professor Copeland's window before crossing the grass to Mower. Philip climbed the steps to the suite of rooms he and Presley shared, a sitting room, two bedrooms, a study, and a bathroom, luxurious compared with the space he had rented on Holyoke Street before the war, or the year he'd dormed in Thayer, a room heated by a coal grate.

Philip stood on the threshold of the sitting room. The firedogs, a contribution from Mr. Alston, who had purchased them new as a freshman thirty-five years earlier, opened their sooty mouths in silent greeting. Philip switched on the table light. Its green shade brightened. Mrs. Alston had sent a sofa and a Morris chair to go with the other furnishings Presley had accumulated. Paintings of clipper ships filled one wall. Philip went into his bedroom and lay down in the dark.

~

"So listen . . ." Presley was saying.

Philip had met Presley at the Varsity Club. After dinner they sipped coffee and watched Sedgwick, who played tackle, shoot billiards with Phinney.

"I'm thinking of a visit to a lady who is widely appreciated for understanding what men like. Interested?"

"I'm tired," Philip said.

"Mrs. Dunn's will pep you up. Just the ticket, I promise."

Philip shook his head.

"We might go to Locke's later on."

"Pooch said I have to be fast tomorrow. I'd better have an early night," Philip answered.

"Then I'll try to be quiet when I come in."

The two finished their coffee and walked outside to Quincy Street. Philip helped Presley raise the roadster's top.

"Enjoy yourself."

"You know I will," Presley said.

Philip returned to Mower. After a while the custodian knocked on the door and told Philip he had a phone call.

"Who is it?"

"She didn't say, sir."

Philip followed the man downstairs and cautiously said hello into the phone.

"I know when we can see each other. "

Philip thought he recognized the voice, but the connection was staticky.

"Is this Lily?"

"Of course it is. I suppose you have many admirers calling all the time."

"Yes. Several."

"Charlotte's giving a party. She's Esther's sister. Esther's my best friend. The party is after your first game. Saturday night. On Brattle Street. Presley's going."

"I haven't been invited," Philip said.

"You will be."

Philip wasn't sure he wanted to be.

"I'm a very good dancer," Lily added.

"I'm not."

"Doesn't matter. We can go outside and neck. You can do that, I bet."

"Lily . . ."

"I'll wear something you'll like."

". . . don't you think you should be flattering someone else?"

"Someone closer to my own age, you mean?"

Philip didn't want to be rude and agree with her. He didn't know what to say.

"Philip, are you still there?"

"I'm sorry."

"If you receive an invitation, promise you'll go."

"If Presley goes, I will too. That's the most I can promise."

"Good. It's settled then. I'm invited because I'm Esther's friend. Don't mention anything about me to Presley."

~

The woman Mrs. Dunn had introduced to Presley was named Mina Kincaid. He leaned over now pushing his foot in its white wool sock into his shoe. Around him the other players joked and slapped each other's shoulder guards, but Presley heard only the slide of silk across smooth brown skin.

"Let's go. Let's go," one of the assistants shouted. Presley laced his cleats and followed the other players down the wooden steps, out into the sunlight.

"Let's see how much you remember," Coach Fisher said after Pooch had supervised the stretching and warm-ups. Coach sent the linemen in one direction and the backs in another to go over fundamentals.

The tackling dummies were stuffed hard and sewn up tight. Philip had forgotten how quickly they could make your chest and shoulders sore.

"You're letting the thing do what it wants. Charge and follow through. Don't wrestle with it. In the gut. In the gut," Fisher yelled. Philip grimaced, rose off the ground, and jogged to the end of the line to await his next turn. Malone, a sophomore from Groton, stood in front of him, his helmet off, sweat sparkling in his blond hair, his body supple and surprisingly strong for someone so lean. Philip guessed the sophomore was fast, too.

Malone fastened his chin strap and took off from his stance. He hit the dummy in the middle and drove it down. Just the way Coach Fisher wanted. Philip charged and the dummy went down again. "Not bad," the coach said. Pooch gave Philip a nod of approval on his way back to the line.

"Take a lap," Coach Fisher shouted after two more tackles. The linemen broke into a run in the direction of the backs, who were already circling the stadium on the cinder track.

Now Coach Fisher sent the ends to work with the backs throwing passes. "We're going to keep it simple like Haughton used to, but we're going to use the pass more than he did," said Miller, an assistant.

The centers were still with the other linemen, so Miller underhanded the ball to the back. The end ran a pattern downfield. Eddie Casey, Murray, and Presley were doing most of the throwing. Church and Felton were doing some too. Murray would probably start at quarterback, but Felton was almost as good.

Casey's first throw sailed over Philip's head. Casey was a better runner than passer. Presley was a poor passer, but a good enough runner and an accurate kicker. Malone sprinted downfield and Murray floated the ball into his hands. Malone was faster than Philip had estimated. He would have a hard time beating him in a race. Being fastest man on the team hadn't mattered to Philip before, but now it annoyed him that he probably wasn't anymore. Malone annoyed him. Pooch was letting everyone tire himself out. The race would be at the end of morning's drill. Fresh speed didn't matter as much as how a man could run when he had been playing awhile. Haughton believed conditioning won more games than skill, and he'd hired Pooch to push his players. They had proved the point, winning most of their games. Coach Fisher was following the same plan.

The morning was hot for September, the air muggy. Managers were kept busy ladling out water. When Philip saw Coach Fisher and Pooch talking together, he guessed race time was near and waved off the water.

"This way, gentlemen," Pooch said. He had a wide Irish face and white hair clipped short. He ran the centers first, following them with his intense green eyes as they ran the quarter-mile track around the stadium back to the starting line. Pooch, Coach Fisher, and the assistants clicked their stopwatches.

The guards and tackles ran together, then the backs, everyone in a separate lane. Choosing places took time and made Philip jumpy.

"Now we're going to see how it's done," Pooch said, lining up the ends. Besides Philip, Phinney, Malone, and Desmond, there were two others who would probably be sent to the second varsity by the time the season started.

Philip selected the inside lane because he wanted to be farthest back and let the others have their starting marks ahead of his. Malone chose the outside lane, which put him in front. Phinney ended up in the second lane.

"Gentlemen, ready, set . . . go."

Philip took off. His body felt light and his motion effortless, then the adrenaline surge gave him a brief sweat of nausea before he smoothed into his stride and his breathing evened out.

A few yards beyond the first curve, Philip passed Desmond, Phinney, and the other two. He was gaining on Malone, but not by much. In the middle of the backstretch he trailed Malone by five yards. When Malone heard Philip behind him, he was into the next-to-last curve and picked up the pace. Philip matched him but was trailing by three yards with fifty to go. He heard his own breathing and the yells of the team at the finish line. He drew even with Malone and for a second congratulated himself. But in that second he slipped the pace a notch slower and Malone went ahead. Malone was still ahead and Philip stumbled trying to turn up the pace again. Malone crossed the finish line first.

The team began to jog toward the locker room. Malone followed. Philip glanced over at Pooch, who was writing down the times in his training book. Pooch noticed Philip and shrugged. They liked each other.

~

The players finished their meal at the Varsity Club and wandered back to their rooms to rest for an hour before afternoon practice. The custodian had laid out a few newspapers, some a week old. Philip took a couple on his way upstairs. He sat in a chair reading an account in the *Boston Transcript* of a mob in Knoxville storming a jail to seize a Negro named Maurice Mayes, who was accused of killing a white woman.

"I didn't wake you last night, did I?" Presley asked.

Philip shook his head and continued reading.

"You appeared a little sluggish on the homestretch. I thought maybe it was my fault."

"Have a good time?"

"The lady I met was different. I'll put it that way."

Presley walked over to the window. A Packard like his father's car disappeared up Garden Street. Presley remembered Arthur, his uncle. His father found a way to reduce Arthur's inheritance to encourage Arthur to change his ways, to give up the woman he escorted to restaurants and theaters while his wife stayed home and drew the curtains every evening at five.

Presley wondered how many other men Mina saw. Old men like Arthur? He wondered where she lived. None of the women lived at Mrs. Dunn's. She didn't run a house in that sense; she invited certain ladies and gentlemen to visit her residence. What those visitors did to entertain themselves under her roof wasn't any concern of hers.

Presley kept his face to the window. "What are you reading about?" he asked. He winked at his reflection.

"A colored man," Phil answered.

"Phil, are colored men more endowed than we are?"

"Why are you asking me?"

"You're from the South. You've been around them more than I have."

"Pres, I have no idea."

"If they are, I guess colored women would expect more. A white woman might get interested in one of them, too."

"Might," Philip said. He wondered why Presley was smiling.

"Where did you get it?" Esther asked.

The brown suit of men's clothes had belonged to Presley a long time ago. One of the servant's children had worn it once. Lily discovered the coat and trousers hanging in a closet with some of her mother's forgotten gowns.

"A shop in Scollay Square," Lily said, hoping her friend would believe her.

"You didn't."

"Where do you think I acquired this?" Lily held up a necktie and admired it. Originally the clothes had been bought at Stearn's.

The new shirt and tie Lily laid on Esther's bed Lily had herself managed to buy when she was supposed to be shopping at Filene's for a hat suitable for Miss Prentice's reception for parents at the beginning of the fall term, a week away. The previous year the Alstons had not attended. Mr. Alston had been in London on business and Mrs. Alston had been made ill by something served her at lunch. To her classmates, Lily had implied her mother was trysting with a player she'd met at a party following a polo match at the Myopia and that her father, after losing to a rival in a business arrangement, had decided to replace his wardrobe and was off to visit his tailor in Savile Row. The classmates repeated the story to their parents, none of whom believed the part about Mr. Alston, whose reputation for dealing with rivals suggested a man who wouldn't restore his wardrobe but would instead get even. One or two parents wondered if Everet Alston had something to do with his brother's misfortune. Arthur's drowning in Boston Harbor was called accidental, but who really knew? Secretly, though, some mothers wondered about Adele, who was still a beauty and had inherited money of her own. She was thought to be cool to her husband, who spent many evenings at his offices on Devonshire Street or playing cards with his friend the Judge.

Lily undressed and put on the suit. Lily had small breasts. This was the one difference between Esther and Lily that Esther took pride in. The shirt, the jacket, the trousers fit loosely. Lily knotted her tie. She had even acquired Oxfords, scuffed but polished.

"You don't know me," Lily said. "Pretend I've just come into the room, or that we're walking past each other on the street. Would you think I'm a man? If I had a hat on, of course."

"Absolutely," Esther said.

Esther's parents were away, the servants gone to bed, and Charlotte wasn't expected home for another hour. Downstairs Esther selected a recording of French songs from the rack in the bottom cabinet and wound the phonograph. Lily took a Murad from the tortoise-shell cigarette box and struck a match. She inhaled, then closed her eyes and exhaled the smoke into the air. When she held out her hand, Esther guided the cigarette to her mouth and inhaled too, the ember at the end flaring for a moment, a blur of light in the mirror above the table on which the Tantalus stood, one of its decanters filled with port, sherry in the other. The stopper tinkled as Lily lifted it out.

"Sherry tonight." Esther imitated the voice of a woman weary with worldly things, a voice from a play she'd seen at the Keith.

Lily poured a glass of port for herself. Esther noticed that the color of Lily's wine in the lamplight was nearly the same as Lily's hair. Esther sighed. Despite the superiority of her breasts, men's eyes were drawn to Lily.

The singer sang of *nuit* and *amour*. Lily imagined smoky cafés, couples dressed in black dancing with their bodies pressed together, lovers kissing at tables in the dark.

Lily put down her glass. "Dance with me," she whispered in a throaty voice deep as a man's.

Esther stood up and opened her arms. Smoothly she followed Lily's lead, not shy when Lily held her closer. A tingle traveling down Esther's spine left her warm. She closed her eyes and felt Lily's chest moving in and out against her own. When the recording ended they slowly drew apart, both a little out of breath.

. . . The rituals of practice filled the days. Then classes started. The woman who handed me my registration form said, on to something else next year. She meant to be kind. My unease returned, a little jolt that warned you can't hide here forever, a tremor like the vibrations of a subway car that took me back to the war again. Sometimes on the practice field the war took over my mind. I stared into space. Pooch would ask if I was all right. I think he understood. I'd see that little smirk on Malone's face, though. I was distracted, not putting as much of myself into the game as he was. He was calculating his chances.

I had no idea what I was going to do after graduation. Maybe work in a bookstore. I liked books, even if I didn't own many. You said there's no money in that. Why go to Harvard and end up poor, every morning putting on a coat with patched sleeves.

You had stayed on in Paris making contacts. You always knew what you were going to do. Your career was bound to honor your family and traditions. Tulliver's grandfather had arrived in New Orleans from Ireland. He died of yellow fever. My grandfather had been a schoolteacher. My grandmother gave piano lessons and wrote music. Some of it was published under my grandfather's name. They died before I was born. You never asked about my family or mentioned much about yours. Presley, you took me at face value, at least I thought you did.

One of the reporters kept watching me. Ellsworth. I didn't know his name at first. I tried to avoid him. I didn't want him investigating me. I didn't know about the detective. He was the one I should have worried about. But what could I have done?

Classes started and the team practiced only in the afternoons. Coach Fisher followed the schedule inherited from Haughton: Players reported at 2 P.M.; individual coaching for linemen and backs began at 2:30 and lasted until 3:15, when the team practiced new plays and worked on blocking and tackling and running signals; an hour later the varsity scrimmaged the second team for sixty minutes; Pooch sent the players who didn't scrimmage to run extra laps on the track. Coach Fisher hadn't made the final cuts yet, but some of those running laps under a sky streaked with evening clouds and full of wheeling birds knew they weren't going to make the squad.

After several scrimmages, a *Globe* reporter wrote that Malone was the fastest man on the team and speculated about his chances of taking away a starting position away from Philip later in the season.

"Don't pay any attention," Presley remarked, leaning back in his chair after lunch and biting into the apple he'd taken from the plate of fruit in the Varsity Club. "The guy's griped because you don't say much when reporters ask you questions."

What concerned Philip was being noticed at all.

"On to something else next year," the woman said, and handed Philip a form to take to his appointment with Professor Hopper, his adviser.

Walking to Hopper's office in Warren House, Philip noticed a man on crutches making his way up the steps of Widener Library. The man turned at the top of the stairs to adjust his weight over the pieces of wood under his arms. Philip saw the scars on the man's face. Philip stood and stared. He thought he was seeing Doyle again. Philip had seen him once before, on Massachusetts Avenue coming up from the subway tracks.

"Ah, the soldier home with the victory," Hopper greeted Philip. Hopper was either smiling or merely biting down hard on the stem of his pipe. Philip couldn't decide.

Philip took the seat Hopper indicated with a tip of his head. Shelves overflowing with books and bundles of paper rose above Hopper's narrow face and thin shoulders. He swung his eyeglasses, dangling from a black cord, back and forth.

"You defended Munsterburg, didn't you? The Hun."

"I wrote an essay about his views for English A, if that's what you're referring to."

"Copey's section, I'll bet. I wouldn't have let you get away with it in mine. I'll also bet being in the trenches made your opinion of the Kaiser a bit more realistic."

"I didn't defend the Kaiser, sir. Only a professor's right to an opinion."

"We do have our opinions, don't we?" Hopper put on his glasses to review Philip's schedule.

"Tell me about the team," Hopper said. He handed Philip his form and signed the schedule without comment.

"We're strong," Philip answered.

"Better than Yale and Princeton?"

"They're strong too."

"Don't be so diplomatic, Mr. Pratt."

"We play Princeton down there. That's always hard."

Hopper twirled the cord, making the glasses spin. Blades of light darted over the pages on the desk.

"Does my interest surprise you?"

"It pleases me, sir."

"Back to diplomacy. I prefer directness. That's my opinion, of course. I read you've lost a step or two and a fellow named Malone's got a chance to take your place."

"That's the reporter's opinion, sir."

Hopper laughed. "Good answer, Mr. Pratt. What's your opinion?"

"Right now Malone is faster, but there's more to playing end than speed. We'll see how he holds up."

"Ellsworth was right about you, though."

Philip shook his head.

"Ellsworth is the reporter we're talking about. He's my son-in-law. I'm not really interested in football, only in what Mr. Ellsworth finds interesting. We don't have much in common. He's interested in you. He thinks you're aloof. Everyone else craves his name in the paper. But not you. Are you a wanted man, Mr. Pratt?"

Philip clenched his jaw. "Nothing like that, sir."

"Probably some are."

"I don't understand, sir."

"I speak of our beloved institution. I think you'll see it. We're changing. Not only are we granting these war degrees to students who didn't complete the usual requirements, but we're admitting all sorts of students we would have refused before the war. We're going democratic. That's Mr. Lowell's opinion."

"But not yours."

"Frankly, Mr. Pratt, I prefer the indifference of the spoiled, overprivileged Gold Coast crowd to the enthusiasm of eager veterans wolfing down portions of Harvard's generosity. Enthusiasm is not a virtue in their case. They will interrupt my lectures and ask too many questions."

"Maybe your reputation will scare them away."

"I doubt it. I'm such an easy grader. Practically everyone receives a B. Didn't you?"

"No sir. C."

"Good man. I respect a C more than a B. It means something."

It means the graduate student who does your grading got tired of writing B and put down C, Philip thought.

Hopper adjusted his glasses on his nose and picked up his pen. "Enjoy your semester, Mr. Pratt. And find that step you lost," he said without looking at Philip again.

~

Walking across the Yard the next morning, Philip asked Presley what grade he'd received from Hopper.

"B," Presley said.

Philip smiled. In front of Sever Hall's stained romanesque doorway the men stopped for a moment, then went separately to their classes.

A few minutes later, Philip was watching the students file into the room for Dean Greenough's American literature class. Two arrived on crutches, one with the empty part of his trouser leg pinned above his knee. After the graduate assistant handed out the syllabus, the door banged and a man in a wheelchair worked his way into the room. He wheeled himself to an empty space at the opposite end of the first row from where Philip was sitting. The seats formed a semicircle, with the professor's place in the center. Philip looked across the room. The man in the wheelchair took a writing tablet from the satchel hooked over the back of the chair and unscrewed the top of his fountain pen. Dean Greenough said good morning. He began by stating that Poe was an inferior writer because he was a bad man; Emerson a first-rate writer because he was a good man. Greenough examined some lines from both, commenting and illustrating his point. The students were taking notes, all except the man in the wheelchair, who had capped his pen and sat listening, staring at the teacher with deep, hungry eyes; all except Philip, who was staring at the man in the wheelchair and feeling a tremor shake the room, a little jolt that made everything go out of focus for a second when he pulled the lanyard and the gun discharged, then recoiled. Philip gripped the arms of his seat. Slowly, slowly the booming faded and Philip returned to Greenough's slow cadence and delicate reading of a passage from *Nature*.

That afternoon, for the first time since practice began, Philip laid into the tackling dummy and brought a grin of approval from Coach Fisher. During the scrimmage his blocks set free Casey, Church, and Presley on long runs.

"Good to have you back," Presley said. Casey and Church slapped Philip on the back. Philip was sitting on the bench in front of his locker, a towel wrapped around his waist, relaxing, taking his time getting dressed in the dim, steamy air.

By the time Pooch came out of Coach Fisher's office, Philip was combing his hair. Everyone else had left. "That piece in the *Globe* inspire you?" Pooch asked.

"Must have been something I had for lunch," Philip answered.

"I'd order it again, whatever it was," Pooch replied. Over his shoulder, he called good night.

~

The invitation was waiting on the mail table in Mower.

"I recognized the handwriting," Presley said that night after dinner. He was regarding himself in the mirror as he tied his tie. Almost every night he changed clothes and drove the roadster somewhere. He asked Philip to go along a couple of times, not to Mrs. Dunn's, which Presley hadn't mentioned again, but to

Locke's or the Parker House. Presley thought Philip's silence indicated he was trying to figure out why he'd been invited. "You're not entirely invisible," Presley commented.

"Is the rest of the team invited too?"

Presley frowned. "Phinney and that Irish crowd are certainly not invited. Otherwise I have no way of knowing who Charlotte knows or has heard about. Or read about. Maybe she wants to find out how fast you are." Presley smiled, pleased with himself.

"Tell me about Charlotte," Philip said.

"She's an Abbot. Her father went down on the *Lusitania*. Charlotte's mother drinks too much and lays the blame on her loss, but she's been drinking too much for years. If you want to pay your respects, better do so early in the evening. Esther will probably be there. She's a great friend of Lily's. You may have heard Lily mention her."

Presley adjusted his collar, brushed his hand across his lapel.

"You are going to accept the invitation, aren't you?"

Philip nodded.

"You'll have a good time. I'll drive us over, but I may need to leave early. I'm sure someone will be sober enough to drive you home."

"I'll be sober enough to walk," Philip said.

~

Philip studied for a while, then wrote a reply to the invitation. The tower clock in Memorial Hall struck ten. Philip decided to walk to the post office.

The man was standing in front of Brine's admiring the display of tennis racquets in the window. He turned around and noticed Philip passing by.

"Phil?" the man called out.

Philip stopped and peered at the man's face. "Jimmy?"

"I've been thinking of you, Phil."

Jimmy Rosen and Philip had worked at the Hub Messenger

Service at the same time. Philip was the first boy who wasn't Jewish that Jimmy had become friends with. He wanted to be an actor and hung around the Bijou Theater as much as possible. He'd been Philip's guide to learning his way about Boston.

They shook hands. "What are you up to, Jimmy?"

"I'm a stagehand at the Washington, but right now I'm on strike."

"You and the police."

"Mayor Porter should have taken the strike talk seriously when he first heard it."

The anger in Jimmy's voice surprised Philip. "You were thinking of me, you said."

"Wondering if you survived the war. Wondering if you were back in college."

"Looks like we both survived."

"I survived at home. Turns out I'm color blind. Explains why I was such a bad dresser."

"You're snappy now."

Jimmy tugged his lapels. "Yeh, new suit. My girlfriend picks out my clothes."

"What do you do for her?"

Jimmy winked. "I talk. She's from Amsterdam. I'm teaching her English. Some other things too, of course."

"I'm glad you're happy, Jimmy."

"In the romance department, anyway. Some others . . ." He shrugged. "Listen, come see a show when the strike's over. I'll arrange the ticket."

They shook hands again and Philip watched Jimmy cross Mass. Ave. to the kiosk at the entrance to the subway. The ground trembled as a train came in. A beer wagon rattled by. Caissons. The rumble of artillery. Where was Jimmy? He had disappeared, vanished in the glare of light that burned Philip's eyes. Some passengers emerged from the station into the light. Philip opened his mouth to warn them, to order them to stay in their dugouts.

He uttered something, something garbled and inarticulate. A passerby veered out of Philip's way.

Philip shook off the memory, calmed himself, got his bearings, and continued through the Square to the post office.

He walked home by way of Brattle to Church Street. He wondered why Jimmy had been thinking of him. He didn't believe Jimmy's answer. And that flash of anger . . . When Philip and Jimmy worked together, Jimmy never expressed feelings about politics. He interests had been food and girls. Philip started to remember going with Jimmy to one of the department stores on Tremont and Jimmy trying to glimpse into the ladies' fitting rooms. Ahead Philip saw a student crossing the avenue from the Yard and recognized Malone.

Philip waited at the corner by the iron fence of the Unitarian church. Malone saw Philip and kept coming, walking faster.

"Out for an early edition to read what Ellsworth thought about your performance today?"

"Mailing a letter," Philip replied.

"You haven't a girlfriend, have you?"

"Answering an invitation, if you must know." Philip sounded annoyed now.

"I heard no one invited you anywhere."

"You heard wrong," Philip said and started to move away.

Malone pointed toward the Common. "How about a race? Right now. You and me. Let's settle this fastest man stuff once and for all. I was going easy on you before."

"One practice or one race isn't going to settle anything," Philip said.

"Oh, don't we sound so wise," Malone sneered.

"Grow up," Philip said and started to step away again, but Malone grabbed his coat sleeve.

"Afraid of the dark?"

"I'm going home," Philip said.

"You old guys, you veterans, you need all the sleep you can get.

Hey, tell me. Were you a hero? Did you lose your little toe in the war? Get a medal for it?"

"Screw off."

For the third time Philip attempted to move past Malone, but he held onto Philip's sleeve.

"Let go."

"Make me."

Malone squeezed the coat.

"For the last time, let go."

"Do something about it."

Philip's fist caught Malone's mouth and pushed his smile into a crooked line, a kind of fish look. Malone's head shot back. When it was dropping forward, Philip pushed him away, but he didn't hit him again. Malone wiped his hand across his bloody mouth.

"Good night, Mr. Malone," Philip said and walked on by.

. . . I remember coming onto the field for the first game and looking up through the sunlight toward the seats reserved for the press near the top of the stadium. I saw you doing the same thing. Bates wasn't a very good team and writers like Grantland Rice weren't covering the game. But Ellsworth and the local reporters had their binoculars up to their eyes. I know you wanted to impress them. Murray had been elected captain and you were disappointed, though you said he was a good play man and deserved it.

Everyone in the stands clapped. It was eerie, solemn, restrained, joyful. The war was over. On a warm September afternoon life was normal again. The world swung a little off course, but it was all right again.

Then Bates kicked off and the ball floated into your arms. Sedgwick and Woods blocked ahead of you. You almost broke free. Then Nelson ran the ball, then you and Nelson and Casey. No one could cut and switch directions the way Casey could. Coach Fisher had to keep most of you out for the second half to make the game fair. I expected Malone to replace me. I saw him in front of the bench, down on one

knee, his helmet in his hand. But Coach waited. I was glad. When Malone finally came in, I didn't mind. The pass Freddy Church threw to him for a touchdown was a pretty play to watch. Malone looked smug about it. 53 to 0 we won. It could have been more. You missed a couple of points and a couple of field goals.

I remember leaving the stadium and crossing the river, how cool the air felt on my face. You were already at the Hounds. I saw you through the window. A cocktail in your hand, women kissing your cheek, men slapping your back. Poor Connors. He would have enjoyed the view. It was everything he imagined it would be. The streetlights were coming on, globes of brightness shining over the Stutzes and Renaults parked along the curb.

~ ~ ~

"My mother would never let me wear this," Lily said.

The dress was an old one of Charlotte's, blue taffeta, the skirt long and modest, but the top, which had been taken in for Lily's figure, fitting off the shoulders.

"She won't know," Esther said.

"What about your mum?"

Lily reached up and lifted her hair away from her neck. In front of a long mirror she posed, admiring the garnet necklace, a seventeenth-birthday gift from her mother. It glowed like flecks of sunset against the summer color of her skin.

"Charlotte has already tucked Mum into her room for the night," Esther said. "The servants will make sure she stays there."

Lily sat down. She took a small brush and dabbed it in a jar of pigment, then darkened around her eyes.

Esther leaned over Lily's shoulder and watched. "Makes you look Oriental, or Egyptian."

"By the way, I bought a hat," Lily said.

"So? I have hundreds of them."

"I mean a man's hat to go with my suit. The one I showed you.

If I pull the brim over my eyes, I don't think anyone will recognize me. They'll think I'm a man. Maybe I'll walk into one of the gentlemen's bars and find out."

"Oh Lily, you'd better be careful."

~

Another passenger already filled the seat when Presley saw Philip dressed in rented evening clothes waiting on the side of the Massachusetts Avenue. The man was smoking a cigar and breathed the odor of tobacco and alcohol into Philip's face as he fitted in.

"Humphrey, Philip. Phil, Humphrey."

"We met before the war, old man. Remember?"

Humphrey removed the cigar from his mouth, reached over Philip, and tapped the ash into the air. "You missed a fine party tonight. Lots of girls, lots of food, lots of drink. Too bad you used up your one visit to our humble club."

Presley had turned off Mass. Ave. and was driving down Garden Street before making a left toward Brattle.

"Foolish rule. That's my opinion. I think a man who's been a guest once before a war should get to be a guest once after a war," Humphrey said. "If he served."

"Did you serve?" Philip asked.

"They wouldn't take me. They said my heart sounded funny. Bad beat or something. Something they couldn't dance to."

Humphrey put the cigar back in his mouth and began to unbutton his coat. "Care to hear?"

"Humphrey, you're tight," Presley said.

"Of course I am. Prohibition's coming. Drink up. Patriotic, you know."

"Get some fresh air. You don't want to make a fool of yourself at the party."

"Wouldn't be the first time. I grabbed Charlotte's breast—excuse me—bosom. Surprised she invited me tonight." Humphrey turned toward Philip. "Would you invite me?"

"Probably not," Philip said.

"I told her she could grab me back."

"Did she?" Philip asked.

"Gentlemen don't discuss that sort of thing," he snickered. Sparks from the cigar spun through the air.

"Humph, throw away that damn cigar," Presley said.

Humphrey closed his mouth and handed the cigar to Philip, who dropped it onto the street. "Sorry," Humphrey said, and didn't say anything more until Presley stopped the car.

"He might have gotten lost if he'd walked," Presley whispered to Philip. They strolled under swaying Japanese lanterns lighting the path to the door.

~

Lily saw Philip enter the room with her brother. He introduced Philip to Charlotte. She was a bit confused about who he was, then she remembered sending the late invitation. She glanced around the room for Esther and Lily. Lily feared she would give away the plot, but she didn't. Charlotte didn't care, really. Her interest was Presley, and finding out if he might be as beguiled with her as she was with him. Whatever Esther and her friend were up to didn't concern Charlotte as long as they didn't drink too much.

Presley saw Lily standing at the end of the room and for a instant he didn't comprehend who she was, a tall woman with bare shoulders. He certainly hadn't expected to find his sister here.

"That dress shows you off handsomely," Presley said. "Did Mother choose it?"

"Of course she didn't, and I don't expect you to mention anything to her."

"She knows you're here, though?"

"I'm Esther's friend and she's here."

"You're staying with Esther then?"

"Presley, enough questions. Mother knows I'm here. Esther invited me. I'm seventeen. For goodness sake."

Presley looked into the mirror again at Lily's reflection. It was like seeing two people. A lovely young woman whose face he recognized and the same woman from the other side, without the familiar face of his sister. One he felt his duty to watch over; the other . . . well, if I didn't know who she was I would flirt with her, Presley thought.

"I'm sorry to be a nag," Presley said. "Have a good time." Presley started across the room. Charlotte intercepted him and led him toward another room, where people were dancing.

Lily saw a few girls come up to Humphrey and start talking. Pretty soon he was making them laugh. He must be saying something naughty. The girls blushed and concealed their amusement behind hands in evening gloves.

Philip stood by himself. Soft fingers touched his arm. He turned around. Lily slipped her arm through his. "There's champagne, or I can get you whiskey," she offered.

"What are you having?" Philip asked.

"I prefer champagne," Lily answered.

"Let me bring it to you."

Philip returned with two glasses. "Actually I prefer Kentucky bourbon," Lily said. "I love the way it burns when I swallow. Champagne doesn't do that. I could drink champagne all night and not show it. In fact, I have."

"Really?"

"Ask Bertha Huntsby. We were at her house. I was fifteen. She invited me to keep her company because her parents were away. They were seeing lawyers about getting a divorce, but we didn't know that then. She had a crush on me. She wanted me to kiss her but she didn't think I would, so she offered me some champagne. Quite a lot of it. We each had a bottle and we sat around drinking and talking all the scandalous stuff we could think of. Every time I sipped, she pretended to. She thought I'd get tight and then I wouldn't mind kissing her. Or I wouldn't remember in the morning. Bertha's never straightforward about anything."

Lily paused and brought the glass to her mouth. Her lips touched the rim. She closed her eyes when she drank, tasting the wine first with the tip of her tongue. She lowered the glass. Her eyes opened.

"This is a long story."

Philip breathed in the scent of flowers from Lily's hair and the wine on her breath. "Please tell me the rest," Philip said.

"Finally I finished my bottle. Bertha had drunk half of hers. She wanted to go to bed. I helped her upstairs and said good night. When I looked out the window a few minutes later I saw her wandering across the lawn toward the dock. Did I mention the house is in Connecticut, on a river?"

"You didn't mention that."

"Well, it is. By the time I was running across the lawn after her, she had untied one of the boats and climbed in. Then the current seized the boat . . ."

"And you jumped into another boat and pretty soon the current had both boats. . . "

"Exactly. Then downstream Bertha's crashed into a rock . . ."

"And you rescued her."

"Sort of reminds you of a Mary Pickford movie, doesn't it?"

"I met her when she came to Boston selling war bonds."

"Truly?"

"Truly. How much of your story is true?"

"Bertha did get tight and try to kiss me. Would you like to kiss me?" Philip had been concentrating on her mouth for several minutes, imagining how it would feel.

"Alice Blue Gown" was playing in the other room. "I'd like to dance with you," Philip said.

"That song's awfully old, isn't it?"

"Before the war."

"I'd rather go outside."

"I'm sure there'll be a new song."

"I'm sure there'll be a new song too, but I'd prefer to have another glass of champagne and a walk in the gardens. You don't have to kiss me if you don't want to."

Philip took two full glasses and followed Lily out to the terrace, where some tables with candles on them had been set on the slate. Presley was dancing with Charlotte, staring over her shoulder at the people on the terrace and trying to pay attention to her talk about tea dances and country clubs and the autumn round of parties. Presley had told Mina he would be at Mrs. Dunn's by eleven o'clock. He needed to leave soon. He watched Philip turn around and hand Lily a glass. They stood quite close together, Presley thought. Lily said something in Philip's ear, then the two of them walked across the terrace and disappeared beyond a tall hedge of hemlocks.

"French women spoiled you, I suppose," Lily said.

Lily slipped her arm through Philip's. They walked along the path. Earth smells. Dry fragrance of flowers dying. A few crickets chirped in the grass.

"You can if you want to," Philip answered.

"But you're not going to tell me."

"Whatever I told you wouldn't come up to what your imagination creates."

"I do know the difference between what's fact and what's made up."

"Which are you?"

Lily stopped to drink from her glass. "A little of each," she said. "You are too. Don't we need to create each other?"

Her dress brushed his trousers as they walked. "Maybe you're right," he said.

"Do you like movies?"

"I see them sometimes."

"I adore them. I wish I could write stories for them."

"I don't think many women get to do that."

"Instead of an amendment for women to vote, we should have one for women to be taken seriously."

"Lily, not talking about French women doesn't mean I don't take you seriously."

"I understand."

"I do take you seriously."

"I think I scare you a bit."

Lily stepped in front of Philip and stood still.

"Please kiss me."

~

A man Presley didn't know asked to cut in. Charlotte pouted at Presley's lack of reluctance to surrender her.

Don't stay away," she said to Presley under her breath. He disappeared among the other dancers.

A few minutes later Esther beckoned to her sister. "One of the guests is in the kitchen and won't leave. tiresome. Cook said to get you."

Humphrey, Charlotte supposed. Who else? She found him drinking her mother's rum.

"Want to grab me now," he mumbled. He leaned against a table, spilling rum and grinning, his eyes unfocused.

"I want you to leave," Charlotte said.

"Amen to that," the cook added, looking up from the cake she was frosting.

"Too tired to walk," Humphrey managed to say.

"Keep an eye on him," Charlotte told the cook.

"I keep an eye on him, but he won't go nowhere less he falls down."

Charlotte searched the rooms for Presley. He wasn't at one of the tables outside either. Then she wondered if he'd gone off with someone. She passed the hedge and saw a couple on the path. The man had his arms around the woman. Her face was raised to his. Charlotte stood a few feet away. The couple stopped kissing and she recognized Lily and Philip.

⁂

"Mrs. Dunn doesn't tell me what to do," Mina said.

Presley liked to lie beside Mina and watch the lamplight glowing on her skin. So many different shades of color appearing, changing, and reappearing. Part of her was coffee. Part of her was tea. Pale to dark to darker to darkest. He breathed in her smell.

The fire in the grate warmed the room. He licked a drop of sweat between her breasts and the salt stung the cut inside his mouth where a cleat had caught him in the game. He had told her about it, and she had put her tongue there. She did everything he asked, until now.

"Please don't try to order me about."

Even when she was disagreeing with him, Presley liked her voice. She had grown up in Vancouver and her accent was slightly British.

"I'm not ordering you. I'm offering you something."

"And yourself as well."

"And myself too. Mrs. Dunn's has its limits." Presley paused. "There's the Bunting. We could engage rooms there."

"Of course. Such arrangements keep the Bunting in business."

"I mean, I could because I can afford it."

"I don't care to talk about money."

Presley pulled down the sheet and pressed his mouth against Mina again. She put her hand on the back of his head and raked her fingers through his hair.

"Is there another place you'd like better?"

When Presley talked his breath was warm where she was wet. For a second she wasn't sure what Presley had in mind. He was an inventive lover.

"It's not the Bunting I object to."

"Tell me," he said when she didn't go on. She knew what she wanted was impossible. Why say anything about it?

Presley pulled up the sheet and whispered into her ear. "Please?"

"I'd like to dine with you. At one of the hotels or restaurants. Or go to a department store with you. Go to Filene's one afternoon.

The Bunting was safe. He tried to think of restaurants, places with privacy, places his father or his friends didn't frequent. And shopping. That would have to wait until the football season was over.

"I know," Mina said. She caressed his face.

"I've never met anyone like you," Presley said.

He was grateful, she could hear it in his voice, and tell it from his body, the way he didn't want to put himself inside her again, not right now, but only desired to hold her and lie with her against him, as if, even in the warmest room, he was cold and could not be warm without her.

~

Everet Alston had spent the evening playing cards with the Judge and two other men. He had parked his car near the Judge's residence. He said good night and descended the steps, paused to adjust his hat, and proceeded along the sidewalk. The wind blew from the east. He could taste the dampness of the harbor. He walked on, passing under the hazy streetlight filtered through the leaves. Presley had described the war lights in Paris. Mr. Alston imagined the city: zeppelins cruising the sky, the boom of artillery. Presley was a good son, a brave son. What it must have been like to punish that man on the boat who tried to betray their position to the Germans, to execute him right there, on the spot. Mr. Alston could feel the gun in his hand, see terror in the man's eyes.

When Mr. Alston came to the place where he had parked his car, the car was gone. He walked down the street. Walked back. Nothing.

He smelled cigarette smoke. A man leaned against the handrail above the steps to someone's house. Mr. Alston approached the man, saw the shirtsleeves and apron he wore. A domestic having a smoke before finishing up for the evening.

"My automobile has been taken," Mr. Alston said.

The man shrugged, inhaled his cigarette, and watched the smoke blow away.

"Did you see anything?" Mr. Alston asked.

"Just came out," the man replied. Not "just came out, sir." What can one expect? Mr. Alston asked himself.

"I think I'd better notify a policeman," Mr. Alston said.

"You won't find one. They're all on strike." The man seemed pleased with the situation.

"Not much help, are you?"

"Not my problem," the man said. He dropped his cigarette end and stepped on it.

"Crime is a problem for everyone," Mr. Alston uttered.

"Then why don't you grab a nightstick and go on patrol yourself? We'll all feel safer, I'm sure."

The nation had mobilized and fought a war. Now there was chaos. Perhaps I ought keep a pistol with me, Mr. Alston told himself. He imagined pressing the gun into the chest of this insolent domestic, having him fall down and beg forgiveness.

. . . What an extraordinary night, Presley, for both of us. Things happened that night that changed the rest of our lives.

I couldn't get Lily out of my mind, nor did I want to. I tasted her mouth all the way home. I lay in bed thinking about her, thinking about you too. I was your friend. No matter how long Lily kept me awake remembering her mouth on mine, or the sound of her voice, or the smell of her hair, or the look in her eyes, I could not allow myself to care for her or her for me.

I was very much in your father's thoughts, wasn't I? Me, the shabby young man at the curb he cast his eyes over, I had been coveting his motor car, hadn't I? Naturally he thought of me when it was taken. I'd know where his friend, the Judge, lived, and when they played cards, and when I might easily take the car myself or pass on the information to someone else. I had been to your house, I had met the

Judge, you were my roommate. You had probably mentioned something. I suppose I would have remained only a hunch, only a possibility in your father's mind as he tried to make sense of his car missing, only a suspect, except for my doing Jimmy a favor.

Anyway, you were a gentleman at first about me and Lily. The rain was pattering against the windshield and you stopped on the bridge on our way to the stadium to practice and we closed the top. Lily had had too much to drink, you said. She was only seventeen. You implied I was a gentleman to put up with her. A gentleman would not take advantage of the situation. A gentleman would not encourage her.

Humphrey woke stiff and sore. He had navigated his way from the party toward Harvard Square. He intended to go toward Mt. Auburn Street but took a wrong turn and spent the night on a bench in the Common. Although the sun had burned off the mist, Humphrey shivered and pulled the jacket of his evening clothes tighter around him. Lincoln's bedewed eyes regarded Humphrey serenely.

A Negro couple dressed in their Sunday finery pushed a baby carriage in the direction of Mr. Lincoln. Humphrey held his head up and walked past them. This way to the Great Emancipator, Humphrey derided them in silence. They glanced at Humphrey but paid no attention to him. An undergraduate making his way home Sunday morning wasn't unusual.

The caller knew Mr. Alston was staying in the city and phoned him at ten o'clock.

"Are you offering a reward for your car, sir?" the voice asked.

At first Mr. Alston assumed the caller was someone the Judge had spoken to about the crime.

"Not unless it's required," Mr. Alston answered.

"Required might be the word, sir."

"You know something?"

"I wouldn't have interrupted your Sunday morning if I didn't."

Mr. Alston gave up the idea that the man was someone the Judge had contacted.

"A reward? Yes. Fifteen dollars." Silence.

"Twenty."

"All right."

The caller instructed Mr. Alston to mail the money to the fund for striking families of police and gave him the address. After the contribution was opened, Mr. Alston would receive in the mail a key to a garage.

~

The hem of Charlotte's dressing gown trailed across the dining room carpet, a muffled sound that reminded Lily of the clothes worn by the nurse who checked on Lily at night in the hospital when she had her tonsils out.

Esther and Lily had already finished breakfast.

"When are you returning to school?" Charlotte asked.

"This afternoon," Lily said.

Charlotte unfolded the ends of the napkin and selected a piece of toast from the silver holder underneath. She left the ends open and buttered her toast.

"Have you ever been in an airplane?" Lily asked.

"Of course not. Have you?"

"I flew in one at Revere Beach."

"Really?"

"I'm going to take flying lessons."

"Your mother approves of that, does she?"

"My brother asked the same question."

"Let me ask you another question. How much champagne did you drink last night?"

"I don't remember."

"Do you remember the name of the man you were kissing?"

"Philip Pratt. How do you know I was kissing him? Maybe he was kissing me."

"Don't be tiresome, Lily. You know what I mean."

Lily eased off her chair and brought over the silver coffeepot from the sideboard.

"Are you jealous, Charlotte?"

"Lily," Esther gasped.

"Lily, I should be careful if I were you," warned Charlotte.

"As far as Mr. Pratt is concerned?"

"As far as I'm concerned. You're here because I tell Esther she may invite you."

~

Philip lay in bed remembering Lily's eyes, her hair, and the way her skin smelled, like the freesias in Mrs. Bennet's greenhouse. I won't break, Lily said when Philip tentatively embraced her. She pressed against him and he held her tightly then and felt her strength.

He imagined a spring afternoon, the camellias in bloom, the humid sky clouding above the treetops along the river, the rumble of distant thunder. Rain wets the garden. The scent of dust rises into the air. After the rain stops, Philip leads Lily to his mother. If she turned . . . if she turned to show her face . . .

Philip threw off his blanket and dressed. While he considered where to breakfast, someone knocked. He opened the door and saw Jimmy Rosen.

"The custodian told me to come up," Jimmy said in a quiet, apologetic voice.

Philip put on a jacket and the two men walked to the Georgian on Dunster Street. Jimmy drank a cup of coffee and watched Philip eat breakfast.

"Would you help me tonight?" Jimmy asked. "I promised to deliver some food."

"Who's the food for?"

"The families of police on strike," Jimmy answered.

Philip ate the last forkful of eggs and pushed aside his plate. "Why are you asking me?"

"I thought you might be interested, that's all. You used to talk about causes, and you defended that professor."

"His cause is settled," Philip said.

"The way lots of people are treated isn't settled."

"You must know someone else."

"Phil, thing is, reporters show up and take pictures. If the people my helpers work for see the pictures, they lay off the guys because the employers are sick of strikes, especially the police thing. Who's going to fire you?"

"I don't want to see my picture in the paper."

"Don't worry. The reporters never print the pictures in the papers. Who's interested, anyway? They try to squeeze a few bucks out of the poor guy whose picture they took, and if that doesn't work, then they go to the employers. They can't get you either way, so you're clear."

Philip regretted saying yes, but he promised to meet Jimmy later.

~

"Bolshies and who knows who else," the Judge said. "You ought to go to one of their meetings. You even see Harvard men there."

"I'm more interested in my automobile."

"Be patient. Here."

The Judge handed Mr. Alston the address of a meeting hall on Atlantic. "You ought to see for yourself."

~

Late in the afternoon an unfamiliar car stopped in front of the house. It had been a tedious day. Charlotte was delighted to see Presley step out.

"Father planned to drive Lily and Esther to Miss Prentice's but his car is missing. I borrowed the Judge's."

"Mind if I tag along?" Charlotte asked.

"Of course not. I've spent the whole day catching up on my reading. I need company." Charlotte wasn't the company Presley desired. Maybe he and Mina could drive places together, spend evenings in country hotels where no one would recognize him.

Lily and Esther rode in the backseat. Miss Prentice's School was in Concord. Each mile depressed Lily. She tried to imagine what Philip was doing. Studying at Widener? She had been there, gone up the wide marble steps. She had heard the rumor that Sargent was going to put murals there. She remembered students sitting at the long tables in the reading room and tried to find Philip. Maybe he studied in his rooms in Mower. She had to invent them. Women were not permitted to visit men's rooms. Perhaps he was walking by the river and thinking of her. She hoped so. She missed him. Philip was still in Lily's mind when Presley stopped the car and she and Esther got out.

"I know a roadhouse that's open. Would you like a cocktail?" Charlotte asked on the way back to Cambridge.

"That's not the sort of place you should go," Presley said.

"I'm sure I do lots of things you disapprove of," Charlotte said. "You're very eligible, you know. We both are. It's a shame we can't get together. We'd make quite a pair."

"This is a difficult semester for me," Presley answered. "Football, settling down with academic responsibilities . . . "

"Oh blah."

"Sometimes you sound like my sister."

"At least she knows how to have a good time. She's quite an expert in the kissing department."

"How do you know? Did she kiss you?"

"Don't be silly."

"What do you mean, then?"

"Ask the friend you brought with you."

"You don't mean Philip?"

"They weren't shy with each other."

"Philip was kissing Lily? You saw them?"

"I observed every detail. Would you like me to demonstrate?" Charlotte looked out the window. The dimming countryside bored her. She wished she hadn't come along. But she had finally touched a nerve, finally pinched some feeling from Presley.

"Tell me what you saw."

Presley was wearing gloves, gray soft suede. She watched his fingers tighten on the steering wheel as she described Philip and Lily.

~

The women in the meeting room shouted over each other. Mr. Alston had never heard women make so much noise. They cursed the mayor and swore at the rich men who elected him. Mr. Alston kept to the shadows in the back of the room where boxes were piled and an old upright had been pushed out of the way. From time to time some of the children grew tired of obeying their mothers and banged on the keys, releasing a tinny sound into the din.

A man stepped from a door at the other end of the room. He raised his hands. The women quieted. The man spoke softly at first, controlling his voice as an actor would.

"Make no mistake about it, this is a sacrifice," he said. "Your sacrifice. Your husbands' sacrifice. Your children's. You are putting your lives down and daring the wheels of democracy to run over you. Know what? The wheels of democracy will not run over you. Democracy is a lady. A beautiful, wounded lady. She suffers like you. She has been wounded like you.

"No, it is those driven by greed and selfishness who will run you over. Those who have too much, those to whom the benefits of our nation have come so abundantly that instead of falling on their knees in thanksgiving have instead the desire only to increase what they possess, to deprive you and your families of the bare necessities, only the cruel intent of driving the wheels across your throats."

The speaker's voice went higher and higher. Now he let it fall. Silence settled over the room.

In a low tone he began again: "That is what this strike is about, giving you more of the goods you deserve, more of the bounty of this country you deserve. This country is your country. The rich have stolen it away. But have courage. Have courage. Take your future into your own hands. Strike and keep striking."

The women cheered now. Mr. Alston was about to slip through the door and leave the building when he saw another man enter through the back.

The speaker raised his arms again. The voices trailed off. "We have food tonight to give," he said.

An astonished Mr. Alston watched Philip Pratt wheel a dolly into the room. Suddenly someone stood up and flashed a photograph of Philip handing out a sack of potatoes and Jimmy Rosen, the speaker, looking on as if dazed by his own oratory.

~

On the way to the stadium on Monday afternoon, rain began to sprinkle. Presley stopped the car, and Philip helped him bring the top over. The engine idled but Presley sat staring at the road ahead.

"Phil, I should warn you about something. Lily can be impulsive. I understand she drank quite a bit at the party. I'm glad you took her outside to walk it off. Charlotte is grateful too. One thing about Lily to keep in mind, she's only seventeen."

Then Presley put the car in gear and drove across the bridge. He didn't seem to expect Philip to respond to anything about the party or explain what had happened. Enough said. Subject closed.

"Humphrey celebrates too much, but he's right about letting you visit the Hounds again," Presley remarked when they reached the stadium.

~

Coach Fisher, dressed in a red leather jacket, warned his players that Boston College was tougher than Bates and would be a handful. Local pride was on the line.

The players ran onto the field and jogged on the track, then gathered around Presley for stretches and calisthenics. When those were finished, Coach Fisher took the kickers to the closed end of the stadium. Malone went with them. Maybe he could do everything, Philip thought, wondering how Presley would like Ellsworth writing that Malone might take Presley's job kicking field goals. Philip saw Coach put a hand on Presley's shoulder as the two of them watched Malone boot one over the bar from twenty yards. A few minutes later Coach stood on the forty and looked on as Malone booted another one. Then Presley kicked and his ball spun off the side of his foot. Presley worked best under pressure. There hadn't been much of it in the Bates game. Wait until Brown or Princeton or Yale; Presley would come through.

"Pratt, pay attention here," Pooch yelled. Philip took his stance and charged at the tackling dummy Pooch had shoved in his direction. He hit the dummy hard and drove it down.

~

Presley was dressing. A couple of the players had pictures of girlfriends pasted in their lockers. Phinney had put up a French postcard but one of the assistants told him to take it down. Presley wondered what kind of stir Mina's picture would cause. Nothing tasteless like the flabby woman on the card, bare expect for some silk fringe around her waist, a man dressed like an Arab beside her with a paper fan.

Philip came out of the shower room, a towel wrapped around him. He had Negro blood, but he looked white. A good man, Presley thought. A man to depend on. A man you could trust your life with. Presley remembered his father saying one drop of Negro blood changed you, made you different. Not Phil. He wasn't different. His evening with Lily had been Lily's fault. She let her imagination carry her away. And wine. Philip must seem a hero to her.

She loved parades and men in uniform. She needed direction. College would be a good place to send her. Their father didn't want that, but he was wrong and Presley would talk to him about Lily. Wellesley would admit her. Wellesley would change her into a woman who would be courted by men of established families. That's what everyone wanted for her.

Presley finished dressing and waited to give Phil a ride. The rain was falling harder now and the wind was blowing the leaves off the trees. In a few weeks it would be November, and winter would be settling in.

~

The man shook the raindrops from his hat, then held his hat in his hand while he waited. The secretary covered the addressograph and put on her coat. Everyone else had left for the night. Mr. Alston opened the door to his office and invited the man to come in.

"This is the person I'm interested in," Mr. Alston said. He laid the picture on the desk. "This was taken last night."

The man picked up the photograph. "Footballer, you say?"

"A good one, too. Keep the picture."

"I'll expect to show it around."

"I've jotted down what I know about him. Where he comes from. Military service. Those sorts of things. It's not much, Mr. Fry."

"I don't need much."

"I assume you'll need money for travel."

"You assume right, sir."

"The South should be pleasant this time of year."

"I'll make my trip as short as I can, sir."

THREE

. . . I meant to keep my word, Presley.

The letter was on the mail table. I carried the letter upstairs. Mrs. O'Connell, the goodie, was cleaning our rooms. She chatted about the weather. The hornet nests were high in the trees. We were in for a hard winter.

I opened the envelope. Unfolded the paper. I LOVE YOU. L

Blue ink. Blue-black. The color of evening sky over the river.

We had talked. We had kissed. She was seventeen. She was sweet. Surely she misunderstood what love is.

But who was I to talk about love? If I had loved anyone, deeply cared what happened to anyone, then you, Presley, were the person I loved. I wanted you to think well of me, to approve of me. I didn't want to let you down. I would have given my life to save yours. I had no notion of how men and women loved each other. I only knew no woman had said I love you to me before.

I slipped the paper into the envelope and tucked the envelope inside my jacket pocket. I didn't want to think I would have to write Lily back. I knew what I should say, but I didn't want to say it.

We played Boston College and won. 17 to 0, I think. The game was as hard as Coach Fisher warned us it would be. We couldn't get anywhere until Corrigan, wasn't it, their quarterback, fumbled and you kicked a field goal. Casey made a long run. Nelson ran well. The sun on the field was warm and the crowd was dressed in bright colors. I wished Lily was watching. I wanted her to see me play.

❧ ❧ ❧

Presley stopped at the Hounds and drank a cocktail, something with gin in it. This hour was his hour. The room with its high ceiling and white wainscoting and Persian carpet and student waiters in starched, crisp jackets was full of goodwill. He had earned praise and congratulations. In years to come people might not recall how many points he scored against Boston College, nor the number of points in any other match, perhaps with the exception of a Yale game, but they would recall his career, his victorious afternoons in the stadium, all his games rolled into one, a memory that would always make him known, make him admired, make him trusted, and that was money in the bank.

In the corner of the room, beside a table and a Chinese urn, Humphrey and Charlotte were gabbing. "We've made up," Humphrey said.

Charlotte's eyes wandered over Presley's body. Humphrey was surveying the room. He preferred to have a waiter in sight at all times.

"How about some supper at Locke's?" Humphrey asked.

"Sorry. Can't tonight," Presley said.

Charlotte turned around. When she turned back, Presley was shaking hands and kissing cheeks on his way to the door.

~

Philip returned to Mower and slept past dinner. After he woke, he cooled his face with water. He wandered to the Varsity Club and bought a sandwich.

Philip took it next door to the Union. He sat in one of the deep chairs with leather cushions and ate the ham and cheese. The Negro waiters, finished work for the evening, walked past, joking with each other. It would be a simple matter to turn Lily away: tell her he was one of them. Was he? Part of me, he answered.

Philip found himself thinking about the Jeepers, how one spring morning a copperhead had raised itself into the room, exploring its way between the wall and the warped pine board where the piano used to stand, skin all bright-penny glistening as if it had rid itself of winter. It now appeared shiny and new, flicking out its tongue, seeking heat, the students frozen in their seats, their eyes white and wide with wonder, not a whisper, the whole room holding its breath to watch what the snake would do. The door had been left open to let in fresh air. The snake rippled across the floor and over the threshold and across the bare ground where later the students found tiny lines, the tracing of its belly, and into the spring grass where it disappeared. One of the boys blew out his breath. Jeepers, he exclaimed. Everyone laughed and no one called the school anything else again. Philip found himself laughing now, found himself at home.

It was Lily whom Philip was telling the story to. Lily whose delight in the story lit up her eyes. Lily whom he wanted to be with now. Lily he wanted to hold in his arms.

~

The Bunting, constructed in the eighties at the edge of the North End near the markets that provided its kitchen fresh vegetables in season, as well as fish, beef, and poultry, employed a discreet Italian staff whom the clientele generously tipped for services. Curtains covered the tall windows of the Bunting's dining room; no one passing by could see in, nor could anyone dining see out. The diners did not look about at others in the room. Each table was small, usually set for two, and screened by the fan-shaped tropical leaves, leathery and brittle at their tips.

"Do we make a handsome pair?" Presley asked.

Mina reached across the table and stroked his bruised hands. She was two years older than Presley, but sometimes she felt much older. In bed Presley was experienced and gave her pleasure; otherwise he required affirmations of his presence, as if somehow this man doubted himself in a way she could not understand. He was afraid of mirrors; people were glass to him. Why should he care how others saw them when he had brought her to a place where to notice others was unacceptable? He cared so much how other people measured him, this man who could have almost anything he wanted, who was as handsome as a leading man, who was educated, who was intelligent, who was physically attentive and experienced. What did he lack, what did he desire?

They finished their meal. A young man with an olive complexion edged a silver blade across the tablecloth to remove the crumbs. The waiter brought coffee and port. She understood how tired Presley was. She smoked a cigarette and enjoyed the silence. He was almost asleep.

They walked upstairs. Presley had engaged rooms on the third floor. A smaller suite than the rooms at his college, she had overheard him complain to the manager.

No matter how tired he was, the darkness of her skin and her white negligees, which he gave her money to buy, aroused him. Even in his sleep he touched her, needed her. He reminded her of a child who is cold and reaches out for warmth, for assurance. From the beginning she sensed Presley's need for something more, something that began in the body but went to the soul. His need attracted her to him. She had slept with him once for worldly things. Once was all Mrs. Dunn asked. She didn't stay with him because he eased the way she lived her life. She was not a woman who lived that way. Yes, she thought as Presley entered her. Yes, I am more than you expected; give me more than your body.

~

Monday a chilly rain fell.

Philip crumpled the sheet of paper, then began again. I am flattered by your affection, he wrote.

No. *Affection* wasn't the right word. Too distant. Too impersonal.

I am moved by the feelings you express for me.

I am moved by the feelings you have for me.

I am moved by your feelings for me.

Better, but not right.

The stationery was sold at the Co-op in Harvard Square, linen sheets with HARVARD COLLEGE engraved at the top. The box was almost empty. Philip scrawled a couple of lines across the page, then capped his pen. It was the right thing to do to write this letter, to thank Lily for honoring him with her feelings and to explain there were circumstances that prevented him from returning those feelings. He promised himself he would buy more stationery later in the week and try again.

Saturday morning the sky brightened. The spectators arriving at the stadium expected Harvard to have an easy game. They were right. Everyone on the team who was healthy suited up and played. Late in the game Church passed to Malone for a score. Malone kicked the extra point too. He walked off the field at the end of the game, brushing Philip's shoulder with his own, taunting him. Philip kept walking and put Malone out of his mind.

In the locker room Murray chalked 35 after Harvard and 0 after Colby. The players cheered and began to pull off their jerseys and pads. Coach Fisher allowed in the reporters, who were more interested in the next game, against Brown, than the one just finished. Everyone expected Brown to play tough.

As usual, Presley showered and left quickly. Philip walked across the river alone and, without thinking, instead of continuing across the Massachusetts Avenue to the Yard, he turned onto Brattle. He walked past the old houses, the ones in the lean, measured Federal style, and finally came to the turreted Victorian homes with their gazebos and generous grounds. He stopped in front of the Abbot house.

The first frosts had deepened the red of the maples, put a brown luster on the oak leaves, and nipped the roses by the fence. A few blooms, the last for the year, hung on dry stems.

Cars drove by. The sky darkened. Lights came on inside the house. I don't belong here, Philip told himself. He turned and retraced his steps toward the Square.

~

When the Co-op opened the next Monday morning, Philip purchased more stationery. A sign propped in the window announced a welcome-home parade for local veterans at twelve o'clock.

Professor Greenough put down the poem of Freneau he was considering and suggested that the poet himself, if alive today, would be eager to attend the festivities. The class applauded, gathered up books, and outside quickly scattered into the bustle of noon. Philip watched the student in the wheelchair pushing himself toward the street. The brassy sounds of horns and the beat of drums vibrated through the air.

A crowd of men in uniform prepared to march. Philip had abandoned his own uniform in Hoboken, where he had been officially discharged from service—laid it on a bench in the railroad station and walked away.

The band took its place in front of the marchers. Citizens lined the sidewalk. From the upper windows of buildings people leaned out, waving flags. Bits of blue, white, and pink paper showered through the sunlight.

In the alley between two triple-deckers, their railings decorated with garlands, a few cars had parked. Philip stopped walking. The shouts of the marchers grew louder. The tuba players blew. Sun glinted off the horns.

Hands slipped over Philip's ears. Drumbeats diminished, the air suddenly woolen. Two arms reached around his waist. He turned. Lily's eyes looked into his. She pulled his sleeve. Into the alley he followed her. She opened a car door and pushed him inside. They held each other and kissed.

The music was faint now. Philip saw the end of the parade, men on crutches and men wheeled in chairs.

"I missed you," Lily said. She was watching out the window too, her mood altered by the wounded.

"Whose car is this?" Philip asked.

"Mrs. Abbot lets Charlotte use it."
"I'd better not stay."
Philip and Lily kissed again, then he got out and waited by a shed at the end of a yard. He saw Charlotte and Esther returning to the car. The street ahead was open for traffic now. He pressed himself against the wall of the shed until Charlotte drove off.
By the time he returned to Mower, he'd lost the box of stationery.

~ ~ ~

In the drawing room, Esther and Lily sat by the window. Outside, under a gray sky, the gardener pruned roses, throwing the cut stems onto a heap to burn later. Lily lit a cigarette.
"Do you want to go shopping?"
"I'd rather go to California."
"Lily, be serious."
Lily pursed her lips and exhaled smoke toward the yellow globe of the lamp on the table.
"I am serious. That's where I want to go."
"I thought you said your father might send you to college."
"That's what Presley wants, not me."
"What are you going to do in California?"
"Meet Mr. Griffith and talk my way into the movies."
"You need a bigger bosom."
"I don't want to be on the screen, and I don't need bigger breasts to write scripts."
"Let's be practical. Let's go shopping this morning and have lunch at Albert's. It'll be fun. The Square will be full of the football crowd."
"All right." Lily stood up and tossed the cigarette into the fireplace. "I want to try my disguise."
"Try it on Charlotte."
"Es, don't mention anything about my suit to Charlotte. Promise?"

"Promise," Esther said, the exact word she had spoken to Charlotte, who had asked her to report any future meetings between Lily and Mr. Pratt.

Esther helped Lily adjust the suspenders to fit her body. Lily became someone she hadn't seen before. Esther was amazed. Lily pulled a hat over her eyes. "Ready," she said.

"The Co-op?" Esther asked when they reached Harvard Square.

"Leavitt & Pierce," Lily said.

"Can women go in there?"

"I'm not sure. Wait for me."

The window lettering advertised tobacco and accessories. An Indian warrior cast in pale zinc held a war club in one hand and a copper leaf of burley in the other. The aroma of Turkish cigarettes floated on the air. Several men, some older, some students, were selecting cigars. Clerks entered and returned from the humidor.

"Be with you presently, sir." Lily nodded, concealing her smile with her sleeve. "Now. How may I serve you?"

"Murads, please."

The clerk retrieved the cigarettes from a wooden rack beside the arrangement of meerschaums. Lily noticed the display of cigarette holders under the beveled-glass countertop.

She pointed. He opened the case and reached inside. Lily kept her head down. "The middle one," she said, tapping on the glass.

Lily examined the tiny elephants carved into the ivory.

"I'll take it," she said. She reached for her handbag. She'd forgotten about the billfold tucked inside her jacket pocket. Did the clerk notice her confusion? She clenched the coins in her hand as the door closed behind her. She blew the Indian a kiss.

"Esther, you need a corsage," Lily said. She lead Esther toward the florist around the corner from the entrance to the Co-op.

"Pick what pleases you," Lily said in a voice as deep but a bit louder than the one she used in Leavitt & Pierce, loud enough to attract attention. Two customers and the clerk regarded her. No one seemed to sense anything unusual.

"This?" Esther asked, pointing to a gardenia.

The clerk waited for Lily to agree.

"Something less perfumy," Lily said.

"Harold, you know I enjoy tulips so much," Esther replied, pressing the gardenia against the collar of her dress.

Lily smiled. Good for Esther. She was getting into the game too.

"You know that's not a tulip."

"It isn't?"

The customers stifled laughter. The clerk shook her head. She was used to customers who didn't know one flower from another.

"Daffodil?"

"Not daffodil either."

"Pansy?"

"No. Gardenia."

"It's not, Harold. A gardenia is red with sticky things that hurt."

"You mean a rose."

"Oh." Esther batted her eyeslashes. "Harold, you're so educated."

Lily sighed. "The lady wants the gardenia. Have you a pin?"

The clerk supplied a pin. Lily found her billfold quickly this time. They were outside a minute later.

"Es, you were wonderful."

"We both were." They hugged each other.

At Albert's Lily took off her hat and put aside the menu. Several customers stared at her. She ignored them and fitted a cigarette into the holder. She held it with two fingers, turned up her palm, and took in the room with a turn of her head, imagining it to be set before a camera, a scene she had written. Places, commanded Mr. Griffith.

"Harold, you're so sophisticated."

Lily laughed and coughed up smoke, her throat already raw from her man's voice.

⁂

The Judge and Mr. Alston followed the usher to their seats.

"I found the car where the note directed me."

"You'll never find out who took it," the Judge remarked.

"Probably not," Mr. Alston replied, but he couldn't put Philip Pratt out of his mind. Philip would know from Presley where he played cards on Saturday night and where to phone on Sunday morning.

The spectators cheered. The teams trotted onto the field. The Judge unsnapped his case and slipped out binoculars. Some of the members of the freshman team were sitting in street clothes on the far end of the Harvard bench.

"There's Howreen," the Judge said. "The man on the end."

Mr. Alston looked through his own binoculars.

"I understand he's the future of the team. Sure to be a star."

"I've heard that," Mr. Alston answered with muted enthusiasm. He was more interested in Presley than Howreen—the present, not the future.

The Brown kicker booted into the wind. Murray caught the ball on the sixteen. The Brown end tackled him on the twenty-six. Nelson managed a short gain up the middle. On the next play, the Brown guard jumped off side. On the third play Presley ran around Philip's end for a first down. The Judge and Mr. Alston applauded.

"Is Presley interested in anyone romantically?"

"I imagine he has his eye on several."

"One day you'll have to face it, another lady in the family."

"Someone I hope who will be a good influence on Lily."

Nelson and Casey carried for another first down.

"Fisher's keeping it simple, isn't he?" the Judge said. "Run the middle, run the end."

Nelson and Presley gained eight more yards.

"If Pratt had blocked better, Pres would have been off to the races," Mr. Alston commented.

"I thought so too."

This time Nelson took the snap. The clatter of pads knocking against pads. Nothing but chests and arms in brown jerseys rising up in front of him. Nelson flips the ball to Murray and is buried by two of the Brown linemen. Another one has an arm around Murray, but Murray pulls away and cocks his arm. Philip sees the ball Murray has thrown right in front of his face and catches it and turns. Breath goes out of him. He feels empty and awkward as he tries to pick up speed near the sideline. Fox, the Brown quarterback, chases him. Philip runs as hard as he can.

"That's mixing things up. Surprised Pratt didn't get away. I thought he was fast."

"Used to be," Mr. Alston remarked, an avid reader of Mr. Ellsworth's opinions.

Murray called a series of passes and runs. Casey watches the balance of the Brown guard, notices how the man's weight shifts to the left, how his shoe bulges out from the guard's weight, then Casey veers left too. There is no one there. Touchdown. Presley kicked the point.

"Presley thinks I should give Lily a chance at Wellesley," Mr. Alston said.

"Perhaps Presley's right. Lily's a bright girl."

"Girl or woman, I can't tell. One day she acts ten, the next day twenty. She intelligent, but she's impetuous. Too full of herself."

Cheers erupt around the men. The ball drops end over end into the Brown receiver's hands, then reappears between his legs, and is rolling over the ground. Harvard's Clark sprawls on top of the ball.

"Ought to produce more points," the Judge said.

Presley circled the end. No gain. Mr. Alston lowered his binoculars and shook his head. "Pratt missed his man."

The Judge didn't agree, but he nodded anyway. Presley lined up for a field goal. The ball floated high enough but the wind caught it and the ball drifted away from the bar. The crowd groaned but applauded politely.

Soon Harvard had the ball again, but its drive stalled inside the Brown twenty. A few plays later, on fourth down at the Brown thirty, Presley's second field goal attempt fell short. The crowd groaned again. The third opportunity came late in the half, and Presley missed once more. "Give someone else a chance," a voice yelled, advice Mr. Alston pretended not to hear.

"I'd welcome a son-in-law into the family," Mr. Alston said, picking up the conversation again. "The right sort. A dose of making do on a new husband's income would bring Lily's head down from the clouds. Sometimes I think she can write a story and live in it."

"Too much imagination."

"College might only make it worse."

"So might marriage."

Mr. Alston laughed. "You could be right."

~

On the field Brown started the second half the way Harvard had opened the first, taking the kick and working its way downfield, but a penalty stopped the march on the Harvard forty. Harvard ran the ball into Brown territory before losing control on downs. As the game continued, Harvard increased its yardage but not the score. Presley looked sourly at Phinney and Philip. "If they score, it's your fault," he warned them. "Play as hard as we are and stop cry-babying," Phinney answered back.

Late in the game Harvard lined up for another field goal attempt. "Who's Fisher sending in to kick?" the Judge asked.

"Malone," Mr. Alston answered.

Malone missed too. This time Mr. Alston was pleased not to hear any applause at all. Brown took over. Church replaced Presley. Mr. Alston lost interest in the game. He found himself thinking about Mr. Fry, what sorts of things he was discovering about Philip Pratt.

. . . We were walking off the field. We'd won 7 to 0. You put your arm around my shoulder.

The locker room was full of noise and reporters. Phinney and Nelson were talking about going to a dance. They asked if I wanted to come along. You ought to go, Phil, you said. You said I needed to meet someone and have a good time.

I phoned Lily after the game. She was going to a birthday party. For a long time we stayed on the line not saying anything, just listening to the sound of our breathing. Have you ever been in love like that?

~ ~ ~

"You don't look happy about Louise's party, " Esther remarked.

"I don't care for Louise."

"She likes you."

"Where's her father taking us?"

"To Vicarro's."

"Where's that?"

"The North End, silly. There's some sort of local celebration tonight."

"I prefer to dine in quiet places."

"Vicarro's will be quiet. You'll see."

"What's Louise's father like?"

"He kisses hands. He's sweet."

"What's her mother like?"

"You saw at the reception. She wears too much powder."

"White as a gardenia?"

"Harold, I loved the one you bought me."

Charlotte walked by the door and wondered what Esther and Lily were laughing about.

~

"I'm sure a little wine won't hurt them, dear. Louise is sixteen now," said Mrs. James, Louise's mother.

The waiter filled the glasses. Mr. James wiped his lips and took up the menu again. Lily lifted her glass and tasted the wine. She studied the back of Mr. James's head reflected in the mirror behind him. His thick dark hair was flecked with gray above his collar. He was seated in the corner of the room, a window above the sidewalk on his right. Lily could see reflections of some of the passersby. More and more people were walking past.

"Would you draw the curtain?" Mr. James asked.

"*Sì*," the waiter repeated. As he started the close it, Lily saw the man and the woman. Lily's eyes widened.

"Are you all right?" Mrs. James asked.

"Excuse me." Lily pushed her chair away from the table and strode across the room as quickly as her long skirt allowed, leaving a wake of startled silence behind her. She dashed across the tiles of the entrance and rushed out the door. She looked down the street. They were gone. Her brother and the woman with him. It was she who had caught Lily's eye first, the smooth brown face under her upturned hat. The next instant Lily had recognized the man beside her, Presley.

"Lily, what's the matter?" Esther had caught up with her.

"Es, I can't tell you now."

Behind them, a waiter held the door open.

"Tell me something. Mrs. James is very upset."

"Don't worry."

They walked back to their table.

"I'm terribly sorry, Mrs. James. I thought I saw someone who used to work for us. I wanted to say hello."

"Really? How peculiar," Mrs. James said.

Esther frowned. Mrs. James's comment annoyed her.

"Lily's impulsive. That's what makes her special," Esther said, trying to put Lily in a good light.

"I hope you outgrow it, dear," Mrs. James replied.

Lily took another drink. She had almost emptied her wineglass. Mrs. James noticed and gave a little shudder, as if Lily was hopeless. Mr. James observed Lily closely, his eyes scanning her face and her chest, sizing her up, imagining what she might be like alone. She returned his gaze and he motioned to the waiter to fill her glass.

"Have you been to Italy?" Mr. James asked.

"Oh yes," Lily answered. "Before the war." Out of the corner of her eye she caught Esther shaking her head. She knew Lily had never been to Europe.

"What did you see?"

"Churches and museums, of course. But what I remember most is the *escupadio*." Lily gave the word her best Italian pronunciation, at least her imitation of the way waiters talked. They spoke the only Italian she'd ever heard. She guessed Mr. James wouldn't know she had no idea what the word meant, if it meant anything.

"*Escupadio*," she repeated, her hands gesturing as if to say there's no translation. The Jameses exchanged confused looks.

"It begins in the night. A celebration. *Baccanale*."

"Your parents took you to something like that?" Mrs. James said. "You were very young."

"No, it was the woman I thought I saw tonight. She went with us to care for me."

"I'd say she did a poor job."

Lily disregarded the comment and continued. "The boats traveled across the water after dark. The oarsmen were old. Young men sat in the bows holding torches. We watched from shore. When the boats were close, the young men stood up. They wore very little. They started chanting. 'Ohhhhhh. Ohhhhhhhh.'"

Esther concealed her amusement. Louise was staring, her mouth open. "Ohhhhhh," Lily crooned softly in Louise's direction. "Ohhhh." Even Mrs. James was leaning forward.

"Then the boats landed and everyone began shouting or playing mandolins or clicking castanets or banging on little drums."

Had she mixed up her instruments and countries? No matter.

"The young men stepped ashore and the crowd made an aisle

for them to approach the balcony of one of the palaces. A girl appeared on the balcony and one by one the men presented themselves for her to choose. Everyone was silent. When she finally picked one of the men, she pointed to him, and the crowd starting cheering again and playing music. It lasted until the chosen one appeared on the balcony beside the girl. Then the whole city seemed to fall silent, everyone looking up at the couple on the balcony. They stared into each other's eyes. They touched. His hand on her arm. Hers on his. Then they leaned toward each other and kissed and kissed for a long time."

Mr. James could see everything Lily described. Mrs. James appeared horrified, Louise astounded, Esther bemused.

"They kissed for a long time passionately. A cannon went off and nearly scared me to death. The music was louder than before and people raised bottles to toast the kissing couple. Then everyone started embracing everyone else and dancing."

"What about the couple on the balcony?" Louise asked.

"We forgot about those two. No one cared anymore. Everyone understood what was going to happen. I mean, what they were going to do next."

"Lily, yes, I suppose we do understand. I don't believe it requires comment," Mrs. James said.

Lily was sure Mrs. James would never let Louise invite Lily to anything again. Good old Miss Prentice. If parents complained about Lily, Miss Prentice always defended her. Mr. Alston contributed substantially to the renovation fund.

"Let's see what's going on outside," Mr. James said after he had settled the bill.

"Tell me," Esther whispered on the way out the door.

"I thought I saw my brother, that's all," Lily whispered back.

"Was he with someone?"

Of course she'd ask. "Philip," Lily lied.

"Oh. Maybe we'll see them again."

"In this crowd?"

People thronged the sidewalk. Music. Smells of sweat and smoke and wine and food. Fire-eaters. Jugglers. Men with dark faces jostled against ladies. Children batted their tiny hands against men's legs. Vendors shouted from stalls brightly painted with figures of joyous saints punishing sinners in burning oil and leaping flames.

"Perhaps they dined over there." Esther pointed to the Bunting.

Maybe she was right, maybe Presley and the woman had disappeared into the Bunting.

The Jameses, clinging to each other, had already walked past the door of the hotel. Lily paused. She couldn't see much inside, only potted plants.

"You go ahead. I'll be right there," Lily said. She wanted to step inside and get a feel for what kind of place it was. She'd overheard remarks uttered in low voices by men her father invited to the house. Then she saw them. Presley and the woman approaching the door, he so attentive to her that he was not looking in Lily's direction. Lily picked up her skirt and managed to dart around the corner of the building before Presley held open the door for his companion. When Lily peeked around the corner, Presley was escorting the woman toward the crowds. She passed through light shining brightly from a window, and Lily saw the color of her dress. It was not the one Lily had seen earlier. Lily was sure of it.

After a rainy Sunday, the wind turned southerly. A blue canopy of Indian-summer sky warmed the city.

"'These are the days when skies resume the old sophistries of June,'" Professor Greenough recited, lamenting that Miss Dickinson was too little appreciated.

Every night Lily phoned. "Philip, I miss you." "Philip, I love you." "Philip, I think of you all the time."

She filled his thoughts too. Water on his skin reminded him of her touch. He inhaled the scent of flowers lingering by a door of a shop in the Square and breathed her in. The rustle of a woman's clothes made him long for her. A flicker of lights overhead in the evening air and he was walking in the garden beside her again.

Mrs. Alston insisted Lily spend the weekend at home, but Charlotte was driving Lily and Esther from school to Cambridge early in the afternoon. Esther had a doctor's appointment. Lily would be on her own for a while. Philip had told Lily that Friday's practice lasted only an hour.

A skein of clouds unraveled across the horizon. Philip and Lily walked in the direction of the Mt. Auburn woods. A bird darted in front of them, a flash of yellow plumage. "These are the days when birds come back, to take a backward look." Melancholy the poem's mood, but not Philip's. The world golden and transparent surrounded him. He could see into the heart of it. A falling leaf, the beating of a bird's wings, a branch sighing: notes in exquisite harmony.

Philip and Lily followed a path deeper into the woods. Among the fragrances of spruce and hemlock they walked, coming at last to a stream. Water frothed over rocks and beyond, past leaning willows, murmuring away.

Philip and Lily kissed. He pressed his hands over her shoulders, her back, her waist.

"What are we to do?" she asked.

"I don't know," he answered helplessly.

They held each other as the light began to go out of the sky.

~

"There's a letter for you." Presley was changing his clothes to have dinner at the Hounds. Philip, distracted, hadn't noticed the letter at all.

Philip picked up the envelope. He recognized his father's writing. Tulliver seldom wrote to him during the term.

Tulliver reported that a Mr. Fry from Boston had called on the Bennets and made inquiries about Philip's character on behalf, he said, of a Boston firm considering making Philip an offer of employment. Some in the company– Harvard men, Mr. Fry noted– had been impressed with Philip's modesty in terms of the press. "Mr. Bennet recommended you, of course," Tulliver wrote. "More I do not know. Perhaps you will enlighten me during your Christmas holiday."

"Seems a Mr. Fry from Boston traveled to South Carolina to ask about me on behalf of someone who is considering me for a position. What do you think?" Philip asked.

Presley smoothed his shirt cuff and buttoned his jacket. "I think the position must involve responsibility. Something international, or something to do with money, or both," he replied.

"Isn't sending a detective unusual?"

"Who said Mr. Fry's a detective?"

"I assumed . . ." Philip blushed.

"Do you have something to cover up?"

"Of course not," Philip said. "I meant something like a character detective."

"These days companies want to be sure who they're hiring. Since the war people aren't willing to take risks."

"Maybe they want someone with ten toes."

"Better yet, nine."

Both men laughed.

Presley stopped at the door. "By the way, in a day or two you should receive an invitation to the masquerade at the Hounds. You'll accept of course."

"Am I permitted one more visit?"

"Just one. You can thank Humphrey."

Presley waved and closed the door. Yes, the inquiry was curious, he thought, descending the stairs quickly. Was there something in Philip's past? Something connected to the colored thing after all? "One drop of Negro blood, remember that," his father had said when the razor fell from the Negro's jacket. The man appeared respectable. His suit fit nicely and his shoes were shined, black as his face. The razor seemed to drop from nowhere and the man scrambled to pick it up, his eyes darting about to see who had seen. Presley's father kept walking, pretending not to notice, as if a razor falling out of a man's suit on the courthouse steps occurred every day. "You can wear the best clothes in the world but you can't change what you're made of," Mr. Alston said and, with Presley at his side, walked on.

Philip unfolded the letter again and read it to the end: "Mr. Fry asked about your family. Mr. Bennet explained who I am and where I might be found. When Mr. Fry inquired about your mother, Mr. Bennet informed him she died a young woman from scarlet fever. Nothing more was asked nor spoken about her. Mr. Fry left the property without feeling a need to call upon me. I assume he returned to Boston with sufficient testimony to your character. I want to tell you one more thing: You are who loved you. I refer to the time when you came into this world. If your mother's people had loved you, then you would be one of them. As you know, they did not. Your mother did not love you either."

The letter ended. But did you love her? Philip wondered. He wanted to have been conceived out of love. At least that.

. . . The weather was warm, not Cambridge weather for that time of year. No one knew how strong Virginia might be. Not Cambridge weather, Virginia weather, Ellsworth wrote. Upset in the air. We'd better take Virginia seriously. In eight minutes we were two scores ahead. So much for Ellsworth's warning. He should have warned us about the lineman who drove his shoulder into your knee, a late hit that put you out of the game. I felt I owed it to you to pay him back. The next play I got him with a forearm. After the game you said you appreciated what I had done. But I knew you well enough to know you were blaming me. If I had blocked the man in the first place, he

wouldn't have hurt you. Paying him back was the least I could do to make up for my mistake. I was starting to notice how often you thought in terms of what I owed you. We were ahead by six touchdowns when Fisher let Malone kick a forty-yarder. I suppose Fisher wanted to find out how strong Malone's leg was. He didn't think he could kick that far. I didn't either. The press hanging around Malone congratulating him made you angry. You deserved better.

Fisher praised us for our team play. Maybe he was right about the others, but sometimes I played for myself. I liked being the outsider, the man at the end of the line, the player who had a different story to tell than the one people thought he told when they saw the color of his skin.

His knee too swollen to drive, Presley drank his cocktails and called for a taxi to take him to the North End. Mina was waiting. She wished to be escorted to dinner somewhere else, not hidden behind the foliage in the Bunting's dining room. I can hardly move, Presley explained. I bet you can lying down, she teased, and put him in a better mood. She convinced him to take her to Vicarro's. They sat at a table away from the windows.

"This is lovely, isn't it?"

Though she intended Presley to think she complimented the attentive waiters, the food, the comfortable chairs, the polished plates, the soft lamplight, she was imagining another life, a future, going places with him. Best of all, accompanying him to the Hounds. Its reputation and rules were as notorious as some of its parties. The Hounds, epitome of Brahmin arrogance. No Negroes worked there, even in the kitchen. Probably no colored person had ever set foot inside the Hounds whether to bring coal or to assist a white man employed to sand floors or to hang a door or to tend the plumbing. Another life indeed. Another world.

The wine mellowed Presley. His desire for Mina slumbered.

The evening air would revive him. Presley was content to be on view, to be appreciated by the gazes sweeping over him.

At the Bunting Presley ordered brandy sent up. He was right, of course, the evening air awakened desire. And right, too, the pain would, at least for a while, go away. In the morning he'd get his car and spend Sunday at the cottage.

~

Mr. Fry sat on a bench in a square of green grass across from his hotel. He had broken off a stem from the bush of yellow flowers. Japonica, the woman informed him when he had asked her its name. He could hardly see the face behind her veil, but her curt reply registered her displeasure that anyone would delay her as she crossed the square to the church, whose ringing bells had startled a flock of pigeons that were now settling again on the ridge of the vaulted roof. I'm paid to ask questions, he said to himself. Too bad if you don't like it. Southern manners annoyed him.

The flower didn't have any smell. Mr. Fry threw it away and headed toward the line of taxis by the curb in front of the hotel. On Sunday morning it was where the fares would be. He had shown most of the drivers the picture already, but he needed to keep asking, just in case someone recognized Mr. Pratt, might have taken him somewhere, perhaps somewhere he ought not to have gone.

"Seen him?"

"Could have," the driver said, third one in line. "You smoke?"

Mr. Fry opened his case and offered the man a cigarette. Mr. Fry propped his foot on the running board, leaned closer to the window, and struck a match.

"Let me see the picture again."

Mr. Fry handed it to the man, who wiped his hand over the face in the picture as if trying to make it clearer.

"Who do you work for?"

"I trained with Pinkerton. I work for myself now."

"I mean, why are you after this person?"

"I didn't say I was after him. I'm interested in information about him."

"Someone's paying you to find out about him?"

"Another party. Yes."

"Someone from here?"

"A client in Massachusetts."

The driver inhaled deeply and brushed off some ashes that speckled his coat. "Of course I'll pay you," Mr. Fry added.

"Have to. Nothing's free this time. People from Massachusetts come down here once before and took what they wanted. Won't happen again."

"I had nothing to do with that."

"What I'm saying is I'm suspicious."

"You don't want to be involved."

"That's right."

"Tell me what you know. Get paid. That's all. We go our separate ways."

"How much?"

"Depends."

"Fifty dollars."

"That's a lot of money."

The driver handed back the picture. "This man could have a lot of problems."

"But fifty . . ."

"I bet it's not your money."

Mr. Fry lifted his foot off the running board. He opened the back door and sat down inside the cab. He took ten dollars out of his billfold, reached over the seat, and dropped the money beside the driver. "We'll act like this is a fifty-dollar trip. You start talking. I may get out if we've gone far enough."

"End of August a policeman got hurt. Bad part of town."

The driver paused. Mr. Fry put another ten by his side.

"And a man named Purdy was killed. Colored man."

The driver paused again, his hands on the wheel.

"We're going too slow," Mr. Fry said.

"Policeman said a white boy killed Purdy and stuck him too. He would have died along with Purdy except police don't go there alone. Another policeman came looking for him."

Mr. Fry floated ten more dollars over the seat.

"Now I ain't accusing the man you showed me, but I did drive that man to that part of town and he went into the house where the policeman got hurt and Purdy got killed."

"Did anyone else see him?"

"Oh my, yes. A lady down the street. She was talking to me while he was in there and she seen him come out and get into my cab. He was agitated and upset and all in a sweat."

"He's the man in the picture. You're sure?"

The driver sat staring out the window, his hands on the wheel. Mr. Fry released a bill.

"One hundred percent. I've gotten to know the lady a bit and I'm sure she's sure too. In fact it would be in her interest to testify to it."

"She's in business?"

"I think you understand. There's a lot of visiting in that part of town."

"What was Purdy's business?"

"He took care of people."

Mr. Fry dropped the last ten over the seat. The driver wadded the bills together and pushed them into his pocket.

"White boys visit that part of town to buy a lady's company or get rid of a mistake. Purdy could make a woman all right again. That's all I know."

"I don't want to know anything else," Mr. Fry said.

"I'm free to drive you to the station. That's where I carried the man in the picture."

"I'm not ready to leave yet."

"Now you ain't goin' to talk to the police, are you?"

"The policeman's all right, isn't he?"

"He pulled through."

"I'm from out of town. I don't get involved in local matters."

Mr. Fry noted the number of the cab and stepped down. People were emerging into the light from the church. The scene pleased Mr. Fry deeply. Virtuous people, breaths redolent with communion wine, hearts full of secrets. He reached through the window and briefly clasped the driver on the shoulder, then walked up the street.

~

"Presley, what a wonderful surprise," Adele Alston said. The shore was usually too far for him to travel on Sunday after a game. She supposed he slept late and brunched with his friends. Since the war she scarcely bothered to keep in mind where he was.

Mr. Alston observed how carefully Presley walked. In the morning paper he'd read about the injury. Lily's eyes searched her brother for clues: a chafe on his smooth skin that might have come from passion not football, something amiss in the way he dressed. His suit, she imagined, was what he had worn the evening before. His handkerchief (had he wiped the traces of a woman's mouth off on it?) drooped almost insolently from his breast pocket. Did Lily detect the whiff of perfume rising off Presley's skin as he bent to kiss her cheek?

"Much fitter," he replied to his father's question about his condition.

Lily stuck her tongue in her cheek. "A good night's sleep helps so much," she said and smiled primly, the way her doctor smiled in self-congratulation after advising her on the benefits of clean habits for mind and body.

Presley returned Lily's attempt at humor with cold blue eyes, no flicker of amusement in them at all.

After lunch he caught up with Lily on the path to the boathouse.

"The goodie tells me. The custodian tells me too. The same voice. The same handwriting. Yours, Lily. I warned you before."

"You said I was too young. I'm not."

"I want to be kind, Lily. There are things about Phil you have no idea of. Trust me. He is not what he appears to be. Believe what I tell you. Do not write to him again. Do not talk to him again. I forbid it."

"You have secrets too," she shot back.

"What are you talking about?"

Too soon to play her hand. Too soon to show her cards. "Oh nothing. I'm just cross. I'm going for a sail," she said.

"Have a good time," Presley replied.

She raised her face and touched her cheek with her fingertips. "I think the sun's warm enough to add a little color to my skin. Some men admire women with dark skin, don't they?"

"I suppose some men do," Presley said.

Both turned around to hide their thoughts and walked away.

All the last week of October a slow cold rain. Leaves dropped from the trees and stuck to the gray sidewalks. Presley spent the week catching up on his studies, returning late each night from Widener to the rooms in Mower. The firedogs greeted him, their heads raised in the embers of the fire Philip had started to chase the chill from the air.

The chill abided in Presley's spirit, though, and each afternoon that his injury kept him on the sidelines during practice deepened his discontent. Ellsworth's column had discussed the weakness of Harvard's schedule. A case in point, the upcoming match with Springfield College. Fisher would probably let Malone do the kicking. If Presley was going to have a chance of making Walter Camp's All-America, he needed to finish the season kicking well to atone for his earlier misses.

Philip would turn over in his bed and hear Presley close the door. The window was open and Philip would be listening to the sound of rain or the rolling of a cart's wheels down Massachusetts Avenue. He pressed his cheek against his pillow and could keep nothing in his mind but Lily.

~

Philip played listlessly on Saturday. The whole team did. Presley sat on the bench bundled up, bent over, rain spattering on the hood of his jacket, and watched Casey and Nelson score three touchdowns. Malone made two extra points and missed the third. Presley kept his head down, hiding his satisfaction.

Most of the spectators left before the fourth quarter. Harvard won by twenty points. Mr. Alston stayed to the end.

Mr. Alston had joined the Hounds his junior year, along with his friend Teddy Roosevelt. The story had gotten back to Roosevelt, about the German agent on the boat and how Presley had taken care of the man. Roosevelt sent Presley his good wishes. Mr. Alston had the letter in his pocket to show Presley, Roosevelt's appreciation for a job well done, along with some unflattering comments about Mr. Wilson.

The crowd at the Hounds was as noisy as usual. Presley and his father took their cocktails outdoors and stood on the side porch. The rain had soaked into the branches of the lilacs at the edge of the yard, turning the wood black, reminding Presley of a drawing he had bought for Mina.

"What did you think of Mr. Pratt's performance today?" Mr. Alston asked.

"As good as anyone else's."

"Casey got off a couple of nice runs on Phinney's side."

"Phil's father wrote that a man was inquiring about Phil."

"Speaking of letters." Mr. Alston reached into his pocket. Presley put down his cocktail and read Mr. Roosevelt's remarks.

"I'm honored," Presley said.

"No more than you deserve."

Presley returned the letter to his father. "The business of the man asking about Phil. What do you make of it?"

"That's what it is. Business. Someone's business."

Mr. Alston sipped his cocktail and gazed across the lilacs at a touring car parked behind the next house.

"That's more or less what I thought too," Presley said.

"Your new car. Still like how it handles?" Mr. Alston asked, looking off.

"I'm very pleased."

"I mentioned mine was stolen, didn't I?"

"Yes. On Sunday."

"I want to catch who did it."

"At least the police aren't on strike now."

"For the moment, anyway."

"Even the stagehands are back at work."

"I guess that means the shows are on at the Howard again."

"Are you asking a question or merely speculating?"

"How are you spending your free time?"

Presley laughed. "Not watching burlesque shows."

Humphrey and another man in high spirits joined the conversation. Mr. Alston stayed a few more minutes, then wished everyone good evening.

. . . I'm superstitious. There's something unlucky about November. Some kind of emptiness in the sky that makes me feel empty. Lily didn't tell me about Sunday at the cottage. We talked on the phone. We have to be careful was all she said.

You mentioned your parents were going to Princeton to watch the game. I wanted Lily to go too. She said she wouldn't go with her father; he wouldn't invite her anyway.

All week long I had bad feelings about Princeton, but on the train going down on Thursday I wasn't thinking about football, only the time before when I was riding in the other direction. The landscape out the window was passing backward, going the wrong way, I was going the wrong way. Instead of the rattle of the cars, I heard the gasp of the policeman's breath. The iron wheels were keening down an edge of steel straight into the man's soft throat.

Two or three times I got up to wash my hands. You asked me if I was all right. Malone said I had to pee a lot. Afraid of the big bad Tigers? You told him to shut up. We were still friends.

~ ~ ~

The team slept at the inn in Princeton and took meals in the dining room. On Friday the Princeton players ate there too, the men from one school sizing up the others. Some remarks were passed on both sides, too low for everyone to hear, but loud enough to add to the tension in the room. Trimble, Garrity, and Strubing, stars of the Princeton backfield, left the room last, pausing to stare confidently at Coach Fisher and Pooch, who were seated closest to the door.

Mr. and Mrs. Alston had journeyed south on a special train arranged for by the Harvard Club. The men around her smoking cigars, drinking whiskey, reminding each other of games long past and celebrations memorable mostly for embarrassing behavior–what did these men find so worthwhile or so important to leave comfortable homes miles away to maintain a camaraderie in such cold conditions? It struck her as silly. She agreed to accompany Everet only in order to visit friends in Morristown. She was glad she didn't depend on Everet. She had a life apart from his. Friends, like Mrs. Gardner. She attended lectures and concerts. She read books. She liked painting. Fortunate too, she thought, that she had the money for her own life, a trust fund from her mother, a portion of which came to Lily on her eighteenth birthday.

Mrs. Alston kept her seat while the others stood chanting encouragement to the Harvard team lined up below. Her husband knew all the players and positions. She listened politely. In the starting backfield besides Presley were Murray, Nelson, and Casey. He pointed out them out. He named the linemen too: Phinney, Sedgwick, Woods, Philbin, and Clark.

It was a drab afternoon, warmer than Boston weather, but the sky was low and gray and the trees she saw in the distance had lost their leaves.

Casey fielded the opening kick and ran fifteen yards. Nelson gained a dozen more. Then Casey and Presley made consecutive first downs.

"Maybe this won't be so hard," one of the assistants said. Pooch scowled at the man. "Don't count on it."

The Harvard attack bogged down. Trimble, Garrity, and Strubing took over. With every carry they shredded the Harvard line. "Jesus, you'd think we'd never played this game before," Clark says, his hands on his knees while he catches his breath. Sedgwick spits out blood. Beside him Woods takes his stance. Everyone digs in expecting another run. The snap comes to Garrity. His arm swings back and the ball spirals over the line. Strubing catches the pass. For a second Philip has a bit of Strubing's orange jersey in his fist. Strubing pulls free. Philip's hand burns where the jersey tears loose. Too late Philip recognizes the play, a lateral. Strubing to Trimble. Philip is the only man who has a chance to catch him. The black legs and the orange stripe churn in front of him. Philip knows he's faster, but Trimble is already five yards ahead. Philip keeps his head up, looking not at the legs he's chasing but the shoulders. Closer and closer. Only a couple of yards ahead now. Philip stumbled at the nine. Falling, he reached for Trimble's shoe top, but slid across the ground as Trimble scored. Coach Fisher wouldn't watch the kick for the point. He turned his back and watched the scoreboard instead. A 7 replaced the 6.

From his press seat Ellsworth wrote: "Princeton easily did what no team had done all season, score a touchdown against the Crimson. The Tigers are a genuine team, an opponent to be reckoned with. Bates, Colby, and Springfield were cannon fodder, boys not men."

The next time Princeton had the ball, Strubing took the snap. Philip pushed off the end charging him and wrapped his arms around Strubing's stubby legs before he reached the scrimmage line. On the play after, Sedgwick grabbed Trimble by the shoulders. Trimble struggled to break away. He groaned and lunged but Sedgwick held him for no gain. When Princeton tried the other end, Phinney stopped them, forcing the Tigers to punt. Harvard couldn't advance the ball, either. The rest of the half the teams played each other in the middle of the field, each squad losing on one down what it had gained the down before.

On the way to the locker room, Presley caught up with Philip. "Have you forgotten how to block? You let their guard sting me twice. I had open field in front of me."

"I checked him long enough to clear you."

"You know my leg hurts."

"Then let Church play."

"Don't tell me what to do."

Presley sped up and left Philip by himself.

~

"Care for a taste?"

The man in the fur coat held out a silver flask.

"Kind of you," Mr. Fry said. The man tipped some whiskey into the cup Mr. Fry had been drinking coffee from.

"Which is your team?"

"Harvard, I suppose. I live in Boston."

"Your team's ride home might be a long one."

Mr. Fry said something but the other man didn't hear. The spectators were cheering the teams again as the players trotted onto the field. On the other side of the stadium, Mrs. Alston was leafing through her program. She had already read it twice.

~

Ellsworth had swapped comments with a few of the other writers during the half. He had recognized Grantland Rice and wanted to introduce himself, but a crowd was always standing in the way.

Ellsworth watched Harvard warming up and wondered what Fisher said to them in the locker room. The game began again and neither team's offense could shake loose from the other side's defense.

"A few carries into the second half and it was evident to all that Casey had misplaced his miraculous ability to change directions and Alston was still suffering the effects of the Virginia game. The center of the Tiger line was more than Nelson could penetrate."

Then Woods crashed into Trimble. The home crowd groaned. The ball rolls across the grass. Philip times his reach, scoops up the ball, nestles it into the crook of his arm, and runs and runs. Pooch kicks over a water bucket pushing through the rest of the team as he tries to keep Philip in sight. Philip has a couple of steps on Garrity. Garrity is faster. Philip hears Garrity breathing louder and louder. Twenty yards. Fifteen. Garrity circled his arms around Philip's legs. The ground rose up and smacked the side of Philip's helmet, griming the air into specks before Philip's eyes. Garrity tumbled on top of him. Dirt and lime smeared Philip's lips. He lay face down with Garrity on top, ear against the ground, the pounding of players' feet aching in his head.

Presley ran Phinney's end for a yard. Nelson managed another yard, his body lifted off the ground, his feet peddling the air, before the orange tacklers threw him down.

"Who's going to kick if we need to?" Pooch asked.

"I haven't decided yet," Coach Fisher answered.

Murray called Nelson again. Two yards, no more.

Out of the corner of his eye Coach Fisher had seen Malone warming up, along with Felton and some other subs, but Fisher pointed to Presley. His shoulders relaxed, Presley bent over and let his arms dangle in front of him. The ball spun into his palms. He dropped it nicely, the bounce the way he wanted it, and struck the ball squarely with his toe.

"Three points was all the Crimson could manage from Pratt's balletic recovery and run," Ellsworth wrote.

Princeton's next drive reached the Harvard forty and stalled. After a good punt, Presley, Nelson, and Casey each try to wedge between the muddied orange jerseys. Fisher sends in Church to kick from the eighteen. The ball rises off Church's toe. Garrity stretches out his arm. The tip of the ball, the tips of Garrity's fingers, the ball turning round and round, spinning and bouncing off players' hands before Garrity recovers on the Harvard five. Sedgwick digs his cleats into the ground. Woods the same. Philbin. Clark. Phinney. Everyone on the line.

"Harvard seemed to wake from its slumber. Twice the line broke through and felled the Tiger backs. The third play netted nothing. The Tiger coaches conferred on the sideline, then sent in Frank Morris to try the three-pointer from the eight. A good choice, it turned out. A seven-point lead. The Harvard season was on the line now."

The ball is light in Casey's hand. He does his crisscross step and the orange defender falls away. Church replaces Presley. Church feints one direction, a simple head fake, but the defender goes for it and the yard lines flash by under Church's feet. Then Casey again, then Church. Back and forth. Run the line, run the ends. Then the pass. The ball floating in sky. Casey catches the ball in full stride.

"Then came Harvard's five minutes of real football. In a series of dazzling runs by Casey and Freddy Church, who had just entered the game for Alston and was, therefore, fresh, Harvard proceeded to take the ball straight down the field. With the oval on his own 30-yard line, Felton, who had replaced a weary Murray at quarter, tossed a pass that Casey took at top speed and then proceeded to cover nearly 40 yards, almost breaking into the clear."

Philip can see it in the defender's eyes, the way he's looking at the middle of the line, he expects a run again. But the ball is in the air again and the defender has a chance at it and Casey is breaking out behind Philip who gets his shoulder into the defender before the ball and Casey and the defender collide, pushing him away, as the ball settles into Casey's hands, as everyone on the Harvard bench throws helmets into the air, as the cheering rises up from the Harvard side into sustained ovation. One point behind.

"Princeton's goal was 33 yards away, but Harvard in seven plays covered every yard. First a pass to Casey, then several line plunges, and the stage was set. With the ball on the four-yard line on third down, and everyone in the stands expecting a drive into the line, Felton picked out Casey and tossed him a pass, good for a touchdown. Fisher sent in Malone. In his first big game under pressure, the young man calmly booted the ball through the goalposts and tied the score."

~

Mr. Fry took out his handkerchief and wiped his lips as he watched Philip walking across the field in the slant of November light.

Philip returned to the inn. He ordered a whiskey at the bar. He could hear the celebration in one of the private rooms.

"Didn't I watch you today? Pratt. End. Am I correct?"

Philip smiled politely at the man standing at the bar finishing a Canadian whiskey.

"Let me buy you another," the man said.

"One is all I need right now," Philip said, putting down his glass and walking away.

"I'll have another then," the man said.

The bartender poured the drink and handed the man his check. The man signed his name and room number, and added a tip.

The barman examined the signature. "Thanks so much, Mr. Fry. Very generous."

~

"Miss Lily, you're going to put us in a lot of trouble."

Esther agreed with Walter, but going along with Lily's idea was better than smoking cigarettes and talking all evening. Walter opened the door and the young ladies took their seats in the back of Mr. Alston's car.

"You know where Vicarro's is?"

"I know where the Bunting is too," Walter replied.

He parked across the street from the restaurant. "I'll wait in the car," Esther said.

"Es, you promised."

"All right."

No doorman opened the Bunting's door. "It's like a jungle in here," Esther said. They crossed the small lobby to the reception desk.

A man in a blue coat sat behind the counter reading a magazine. Lily saw the picture of a boxer, fists raised, a trim mustache above thin lips. The man stuffed the magazine under the counter.

"I've forgotten Mr. Alston's room number," Lily said.

The clerk was young and had smooth pink cheeks. He opened his mouth to reply and hesitated.

"Mr. Alston is my brother," Lily said.

"Oh. He hasn't come in tonight," the man said.

"We know. He's not the one we wish to speak with."

The man glanced over his shoulder at the key boxes on the wall. "It's 311. Just knock."

Lily and Esther climbed the stairs, the runners frayed to fibers. The gas fixtures had been replaced with electric globes. They cast a dim sepia light along the hallways.

311. Lily tapped on the door. She heard the rustle of a skirt. The door opened. The face of the woman Lily had seen before now looked back at her.

"I'm Presley's sister. This is my friend Esther Abbot. We wish to speak with you."

More amused by Lily's directness than surprised by a visit from someone in Presley's family, Mina stepped aside. Lily walked in, and Esther followed. Mina closed the door.

"I'm Mina Kincaid," the woman said. "I was going to order supper. Would you join me?"

"We don't have time," Lily said.

"You haven't told me your name."

"Lily."

"Lily. Yes. It fits you."

Lily saw an open bottle of wine and cigarettes on the table by the window. An evening dress lay across the cushions of the settee.

"I'd like a glass of wine," Lily said.

"And what about Esther?"

"Please," Esther said, unable to keep from staring at the woman's eyes, which seemed almost golden in the room light, unable to resist admiring the delicate shadings and tones of Mina's skin, the jut of her cheekbones, the line of her jaw.

"Please sit down. I'll find some glasses," Mina said.

She opened the sideboard, its veneer peeling, and took out two glass that didn't match. She poured some claret. Esther sat down on the settee, Lily on one of the chairs by the table.

"Do you know about me from Presley?"

"I saw you the night of the celebration. We were dining down the street."

"Ah." Mina sipped her wine. "And why are you here?" she asked, the curve of her lips still showing more amusement than concern. "You're old enough to understand the relationship I have with your brother," she said, testing Lily with her own directness.

"I understand why he's attracted to you."

"For now, at least. Eventually someone from his own world will catch his eye. Is that what you want to know?"

"My family didn't send me, if that's what you want to know."

Mina enjoyed Lily's answer.

Mina offered Lily and Esther cigarettes. Lily fitted one into her holder.

"What is it then?" Mina asked. "Why are you here?"

"I wanted to show Esther how . . ." Lily paused. She continued, "how exquisite you are." The words came out on their own, her voice low and soft, not the answer she had given to Esther hours before, but now she realized it was the reason for coming to the hotel, not merely to confirm the woman's existence, nor to find out her name, but to show Esther how beautiful Mina was and see her again herself.

Light glistened in the corner of Mina's eye. "You're kind. I'm not surprised. Your brother has been generous to me."

"Lunch at Parker House?"

"No."

"Dinners downstairs?"

"Yes."

"There's an enormous party at Presley's club in a few weeks. I'd love to sneak you in."

"I've heard about the parties. I don't think I would be welcome there."

"You might change your mind. Do you have a telephone?"

"I can give you a number where you can reach me."

"I'd like that."

"I'd like that too," Mina said.

FOUR

. . . On Monday in his column Ellsworth wondered who Coach Fisher would have chosen to kick if by some chance we had one more field goal attempt to win the game. Malone or you?

We knew he wanted Malone. Malone was acting very cocky now. It didn't help your attitude that Coach planned to rest you against Tufts to make you healthy for Yale.

Tufts had beaten us in the game before the war, you reminded me. Then you said you didn't think about the war very much anymore, but you dreamed the other night about Paris. You asked if I remembered Annette. You asked if I had gone to bed with her. Once, I said. Which was true and not true. I guess you knew that. What you were thinking, I couldn't imagine. Your expression never changed.

You inquired if I had accepted the invitation to the masquerade at the Hounds. I answered I wasn't sure I wanted to go. The first masquerade after the war, you don't want to miss that, you said.

The rumor was going around we would be asked to go to California and play a western team in January if we beat Tufts and Yale. Fisher told us not to count on going. Even if we beat Yale, President Lowell wasn't likely to approve the trip. But I looked up and saw Lowell dressed in his topcoat, hands behind his back, watching us scrimmage. You saw him too. You had your mind set on California.

The air was cold and the smoke from the factories hung in the sky. The shapes of zeppelins. I thought about the muted Paris nights, about meeting Annette by the linden trees, Connors not touching her hand, then that time after the war at the Crillon. You always said gentlemen keep secrets, especially their own. Was that what I was doing, being a gentleman? It never crossed my mind you hadn't had the dream and hadn't told the truth in your letter.

∾ ∾ ∾

Mr. Alston told Mr. Fry to meet him at his office on Saturday afternoon. Mr. Alston was skipping the game. Presley would be on the bench, along with most of the regulars. No reason to get chilled watching the seconds play.

"Oh, I imagine Pratt is quite capable of thieving your automobile," Mr. Fry responded.

Mr. Fry repeated the story the driver had told him. "I believe Pratt had a woman in trouble and wanted Purdy's help. Purdy wouldn't cooperate. Maybe he wanted more money. Pratt lit into him. Beat him savagely."

While he listened Mr. Alston stared out his window past the *Globe* building in the direction of the Old State House. Generations of Alstons had served in it. One of his cousins was the architect of the Lawrence building up the street. The rule of orders and laws, that's what the family was about. Service. Friendships didn't always follow. Presley's misguided friendship with this Pratt had gone on too long.

"You've certainly satisfied me on the issue of Mr. Pratt's character," Mr. Alston said. He let the curtain fall and sat down to write a bank draft for Mr. Fry's services. Mr. Fry laid a folder on the desk, details of expenses and conversations.

"I didn't interview the policeman who found the body. I can arrange it, though."

"Then you know his name?"

"And a bit about him."

"I may need you again."

The men shook hands at the door. Mr. Alston locked it. He had the information he needed. Enough to confront Philip Pratt, enough to make him withdraw. He could leave Harvard after the semester with the credits for a war degree and go away. Disappear.

On the way home, Mr. Alston drove past the entrance to the

Globe building. The game would be over now. Ellsworth would be inside writing his copy.

~

Malone had scored a touchdown and kicked two points. After the game, he brushed past Philip as they walked toward the lockers. When Pooch handed Murray the chalk, someone yelled, "Let Malone do it." Murray kept the chalk and filled in the Harvard boxes with 23, the Tufts space with 0.

At the Hounds, Presley fortified himself for his trip to the Bunting. The roadster leaked cold air. He ordered an extra cocktail.

"Are you going to escort me to the masquerade?" Charlotte asked when she had a chance to talk to Presley alone.

"What about Humphrey?"

"I want someone who won't pass out."

"All right."

"What did you say?"

"I asked you to go with me."

Charlotte was so excited that she didn't mind Presley kissing her quickly on the cheek and excusing himself for another engagement.

~

Presley hadn't visited Mina for over a week. "I thought you'd forgotten me," she said.

Presley took his mouth from Mina's skin. "I've been thinking of you all the time."

"One can almost feel your thoughts," she said, letting her fingernails graze Presley's cheek.

Presley ordered supper sent to their room. "Next Saturday is Yale weekend," he explained. "My father asked me to celebrate with him that evening."

Mina inserted her fork into the lobster's claw and dipped the meat into the bowl of drawn butter.

"You're right," she said. "Your lobsters are much sweeter than the ones we ate in Canada."

"You don't mind, then, being alone on Saturday?"

"I would enjoy a party," Mina said. "Any woman would on a Saturday night. There are probably many parties at the college."

"There are."

"Is your father taking you to one?"

"He has an evening planned with some old classmates. Most of them will probably drink too much and I'll have to drive them home."

"I assumed such men employed their own drivers."

"Some do."

"What about your family?"

"We have a man named Walter."

"I know so little about your family. Have you any brothers or sisters?"

"A sister."

Between bites Mina drew the tines of the fork across the tip of her tongue. Presley imagined the taste of her mouth, slightly fishy, salty, and sweet and slippery from the butter.

"What's she like?"

In her room at Esther's house, Lily had put on her suit and fitted the brim of the hat low over her brow. Mrs. Abbot was asleep and the servants had gone away to Saturday-night engagements of their own, leaving only the housekeeper to tend to Mrs. Abbot if she woke and required another toddy. Esther had driven off with friends to a showing of *When the Clouds Roll By.*

Lily buttoned her overcoat, one of Presley's old ones, the hem touching her ankles as she walked down Brattle to Church Street. She was passing the garage where Presley kept his car when Charlotte came out of the restaurant across the street. She had her arm around a man and was guiding him unsteadily, both of them laughing. Charlotte glanced in Lily's direction. Lily kept walking.

Minutes later she crossed Massachusetts Avenue. Some students strolling through the gate from the Yard said hello.

"Lily needs work," Presley answered.

"You make your sister sound like a carriage or an automobile. Something to tinker with."

"Discipline. Reason. She lacks those qualities."

Outside Mower, two Yard cops were talking. Lily bunched the sides of the coat under her arm to raise the hem so they would see her trousers and shoes. Walking close to the men, her head down, she pushed the door open. Quickly she crossed the lobby to the stairs. She tapped on Philip's door.

Presley bent forward and lifted a curl of Mina's hair. She inclined her face away from his.

"Your sister gets carried away then? Of course, you never do."

"She's too young to feel about someone the way I feel about you."

Philip opened the door. Lily raised her face. Her eyes. Her smile. Philip was astounded. Speechless. Lily shut the door. She took off her hat and overcoat and kissed him. Then they were embracing and kissing again. Philip had never held anyone as close as he held Lily now.

"She's rather spoiled, too."

"And you're not?"

Presley slid his palm under Mina's robe. "Don't I spoil you?"

Philip had been sitting almost in the dark, only one small lamp turned on, sitting in a chair in front of the fire. The wood sputtered and flared. On their knees Lily and Philip still held each other, their image flickering on the wall, shadows rising and falling across the horizons of Presley's painted ships.

"Help me off with my jacket," Lily said.

She made a pillow out of it and lay down on the rug close to the fire. She tucked the jacket under her head.

Philip sat with his back against the chair and studied Lily's clothes. "Where did you find them?" he asked.

She explained where she'd gotten the suit, tie, shirt, shoes, and coat.

"Do you like me in these clothes?"

"I'd love you in anything," Philip said.

Mina picked up the dessert plate, surprised to discover it was chilled. "What do you call this?"

The simplest things she didn't know. To teach her pleased Presley.

"I can't imagine what trouble we'd be in if anyone finds us here. I'll be expelled," Philip said.

"But no one cares what Presley does as long as he does it somewhere else."

"He has certain friends he doesn't bring around for the rest of us to meet."

"Friends? Lovers, you mean. I met one. She's charming. She's a Negro. Does he ever mention her?"

Philip stared at Lily. Of course, now it made sense, Presley asking if Negro men were more endowed than white men, asking Philip because he was from the South and ought to know. And Annette too. Presley asking Philip if he had gone to bed with her. He had lied about not seeing her again. Philip was sure of it. Presley pretending he didn't know Philip wasn't as white as he was.

"Philip, what's wrong?"

"Does it matter?" he managed to ask, "about the woman–what color she is?"

Lily interrupted. "Of course it matters."

Lily hugged Philip and kissed him again.

"Don't you understand? We can do anything we want. He can't object. I'll tell father about Mina if he does."

Lily paused. "But I don't want to. Our father can be cruel and dangerous. I don't want to hurt her. I adore her."

"Has your father ever hurt you?"

"Yes."

Mina finished the dessert. Presley poured more wine, offering the glass to her lips. The English priest, a figure in dark clothes against the white walls of the church, flashed through her memory, and the rim of the chalice as he pressed it against her mouth with unnecessary force as if she were an unredeemed soul whose mouth he would penetrate, with grace.

"Lily, will you go with me to the masquerade at the Hounds?"

"Oh yes," she answered. The firelight shined behind her, deepening the luster of her hair.

"What shall we wear?"

"I know someone in the theater who will lend us costumes."

Presley sensed Mina's mood changing. "After the Yale weekend, there's the Thanksgiving holiday. Maybe we could lunch and I could take you shopping."

"Watching me try on clothes interests you?"

"At the moment, the opposite interests me."

"I understand," Mina said. She had all the clothes she wanted. All the jewelry she needed. And more than enough sketches of the French countryside, the only gifts Presley had bought for her himself and not merely handed her the money to buy. She could make a fine impression on his friends or his family, none of whom, other than Lily, she expected she would ever meet in Boston, that famous old city of Abolitionists.

The square clock with golden hands on the mantel clock chimed eleven. Philip helped Lily on with her coat. She kissed him one more time, then put on her hat and raised her collar around her neck. The night was cold, but a car with the top down roared along Mass. Ave. In the front, seat bundled in furs, the passengers sang as loud as they could. Lily wanted to join them.

. . . Lily and I lay by the fire. All my guilt about not being truthful to you, Presley, vanished, replaced by the pain of not telling Lily. To my shame I believed she might accept Mina but not me. Mina never hid what she was. Had Lily known about me to begin with, she would have had a choice of what to do. Even now as we lay by the fire it was not too late to tell her. Had I known going to the masquerade would reveal our relationship to her parents, I would have told her. I want to believe I would have told her. Instead, I chose selfishly for myself, persuading myself I was choosing for both of us. I was making Lily happy by postponing the truth that would make both of us unhappy.

~ ~ ~

"I hope you've arranged for your costume," Presley said at practice.

"I have."

"And?"

"A cutaway, striped trousers, a tall hat with stars around it."

"Uncle Sam. You'll be easy to spot."

"Not original, but the clothes fit. And you?"

"Someone patriotic as well. Enough said. Are you escorting anyone?"

"Yes."

"Who?"

"Enough said."

~

Although it was the last week of the season, Coach Fisher and his assistants continued to drill the team on blocking, tackling, and timing.

The light faded. Pooch blew his whistle and sent everyone to the showers except Malone and Philip. "You men ready?" Pooch asked.

Philip didn't understand at first. Malone smirked. Philip had forgotten, but Malone had been waiting for this moment all season.

"A mile this time," Pooch said. "Malone, choose a lane."

Malone threw his helmet on the grass and stepped into lane one.

Philip crouched on the starting line in the second lane. "Go," Pooch shouted.

Malone ahead, a pace appropriate for a dash down the field, a hundred yards, not a mile; Philip cut in behind Malone, chasing him, trying to stay even, expecting Malone to slow down, to settle into an easier stride, but Malone kept on, sprinting the first two hundred yards, anger pumping his blood—the fist in his mouth, the missed tackles he would have made if Coach Fisher had put him in instead of leaving Pratt there—past the far turn, then racing toward Pooch at the starting line, Philip wheezing for air fifteen yards behind already and knowing he had never run such a fast quarter mile, past Pooch holding the stopwatch, too surprised to call out the time, eyes filled with the runners, steady on them around the second lap, Malone farther in front now, Philip telling himself to forget the pain, if Malone could run this fast, he could too, Philip telling himself pain was an excuse to quit, a reason to explain why you failed, everyone understood pain, keep your head up, Philip told himself, noticing he wasn't falling farther back, passing Pooch again he was, in fact, catching up, at least a little, blood beating in his ears so hard he couldn't hear Pooch call the time, only saw Pooch's lips moving, a dream face; closer behind was Philip, halfway down the other side of the track; the third lap, not impossible, only one to go, spit stuck to mouth, lips open, sucking in all the air he could, around the curve, legs shaking, shoulders numb lumps of weight, a churn of nausea, but all right, racing toward Pooch again; one more to go, only one more, Pooch waving, blur of numbers, Malone ahead in the turn, Malone glancing back, giving himself away, burning out, spent, pacing himself on Philip's position now, timing himself to use no more than he needed to stay ahead, admitting he didn't have much; desperate exhalations, loud enough now for Philip to hear, Philip ten yards behind, nine, eight, heart thumping, throat burning, whine of wind, whine of Malone's air, desperate, then past Malone in the other lane, no letting up, not now; finishing, finishing, finishing. Done.

Pooch grabbed each runner by the arm. "Walk it off, walk it off," Pooch ordered, hands pushing against their shoulders to keep the men moving.

Presley wondered why Phil, Malone, and Pooch were the last in. Malone slumped on the bench in front of his locker. Pooch disappeared into Coach Fisher's office. Philip wouldn't look in Presley's direction. Philip undressed. Good run for a man with nine toes, he thought.

~

Lily and Esther had taken their time returning from a walk to the village stores near the school. The duty girl had written down a message: I've changed my mind. Phone me. Mina.

The man who answered spoke in an accent. "*Momento,*" he said. The earpiece knocked against the box as he left it dangling from the cord. The man's heels clicked over the floor. How many men did Mina have in her life? Lily imagined this one, a Spanish dancer in polished boots.

Mina arranged to meet Lily at the village tearoom after Lily's dance class. Lily arrived, forehead still damp, a scarf around her neck, wearing a brown pullover and a skirt and her woolen leggings. Mina had ordered orange pekoe and a scone. Lily bit off a piece of scone to taste it. The waitress made a sour face. People shouldn't share. Mina and Lily giggled.

"Does Presley know you see other men?"

"He knows other men see me. I pose for figure classes at the School of Fine Arts. The man who answered the phone. He's Cuban. He's a photographer. Sometimes I pose for him too."

"You said you changed your mind about the party."

"Presley told me there was something else he had to do with his father and old friends from college. But he lied. I'd like to surprise him."

"You certainly will." Lily and Mina leaned their faces together like conspirators and broke out laughing again.

"Will he know who I am?"

"If your costume wins a prize, you have to reveal your face. The others can if they want to. I'm going as Barney Oldfield."

"Oldfield?"

"A race-car driver. The women's costumes don't fit me. See." Lily tugged at her pullover. "All I need are trousers, jacket, gloves, and a hat with goggles. Esther is going as Dido. She played her in the Latin class pageant last spring."

Lily told Mina where Jimmy Rosen worked. "A show about liberty just came down. It had lots of patriotic characters. You'll find a costume you'll like."

"Lily . . ." Mina held Lily's hand. "I'm angry with your brother. The way I wanted us to be will never happen. I can accept that. I can't accept being lied to. But, Lily, I won't go if you might be hurt."

"I can take care of myself," Lily said.

The Cuban was waiting in a car. He drove Lily back to school. He told Lily she should eat more.

The car stopped. Mina hugged Lily. The driver mumbled something in Spanish that Lily guessed wasn't a compliment. The only word in Spanish she knew meant shit. She knew the word for shit in French, Spanish, and Italian. Perhaps now wasn't the best time to use one of them. Lily closed the door and blew Mina another kiss. The car sped away.

⁂

Had she known, Mrs. Abbot never would have permitted Esther to attend the masquerade. Charlotte saw the situation differently. She assured Humphrey she would have accepted his invitation to the Hounds had not Presley asked her long before, early in the autumn when they bumped into each other in the Square and talked about the party over sundaes at the Corner Kitchen.

"Then I shall invite your sister," Humphrey said, his sullen voice implying he was getting even asking someone younger, someone who would be flattered by his attention.

"Do so," Charlotte answered. Humphrey, besides drinking too much, assumed too much. He bored her. Let him bore Esther for a change.

Esther had invited Lily for the Yale weekend. "We're not a boardinghouse for your friends," Charlotte said. "Not this time."

⁂

"What will you do?" Esther whispered to Lily in French class.

"I don't know," Lily whispered back.

"Ladies." Miss Bonnard rapped her knuckles on the desk. She scowled at Lily and Esther before continuing to list the accomplishments of Victor Hugo. Lily wrote *merde* across Hugo's name at the top of the page in her book.

Later Esther and Lily stood by the window watching some of the girls in the lower form dash along the path between buildings. The rain was cold, almost sleet. The girls held their books over their heads.

"In the evening my parents are going out for a while. I'll meet Philip at the Hounds."

"How will you get home?"

"Philip will bring me."

"Then your parents will find out."

Years before, Lily had broken her father's pocket watch. He struck her, his open hand against her mouth. Her skin was swollen and red for days. Her mother ordered him never to hit Lily again. Thereafter he punished Lily with silence. But he would strike Philip, in some way he would hurt him, she couldn't imagine how, but he would, she was sure of it.

"It's not too late to change your mind, Lily."

"Oh, Es. It is."

~

Rain drummed down all week, turning to snow over the hills around Concord. On Saturday a stiff southwest wind cleared the sky. By eleven in the morning, cars and trolleys jammed Harvard Square, tooting and clanging among the crowds surging by in hats and overcoats and lugging blue or crimson blankets to unroll on the cold concrete seats of Soldiers Field.

"There must be fifty thousand here," the Judge said.

"At least," Mr. Alston agreed.

Mr. Alston watched Presley prepare to kick off, the wind at his back. Neville, the Yale half, caught the ball on the seventeen and returned it, zigzagging among several Harvard defenders to the twenty-seven. Braden, a big fullback, drove into the line and Woods hung on, pulling Braden off balance. The next time Clark did the same, taking Braden's charge, wrestling him to the ground. The third carry Braden came at Clark again, and Clark took down Braden again.

Braden punted, a kick so deep it brought applause even from the Harvard side. Casey caught up with the ball on his thirty-two, sidestepped one tackle and managed a four-yard return. Nelson and Presley shouldered into the Yale line three times and gained two yards. Nelson's chin was cut. He wiped off the blood with his sleeve. The Yale guard grinned.

Presley punted out. The second Yale possession of the quarter began on its own twenty-one. Lay, the other Yale half, took the snap. The Yale guard spun Sedgwick around and Lay almost got past, but Sedgwick managed to grab Lay's arm. The ball slipped out of his hand. Philip fell on the ball on the Yale twenty-three.

"We ought to make something out of this," the Judge said.

Mr. Alston had been watching Murray through his binoculars. Murray wasn't moving well, but Presley appeared healthy.

"I don't know," Mr. Alston said. "Yale's thick-headed and tough."

"They're certainly not playing with much imagination, but we're not doing any better."

The Harvard side sat quietly as the blockers tried to control the line and couldn't. The Yale guards and tackles were sliding off, tripping up Presley and Nelson before they started. Presley dropped back to attempt a field goal. Malone watched from the end of the bench. He saw the ball slice to the right. He shrugged and furrowed the ground in front of him with his cleats.

Yale took over, and three plays later Braden punted again. Harvard started on its own forty-five. This time Sedgwick made his block, coming up quickly, taking the Yale player by surprise. Nelson churned past the line, his cleats flinging up cusps of grass. Five yards. Then Presley plunged for five more following behind Havemeyer, who was starting in place of Philbin.

Havemeyer centered the ball to Murray. Yale didn't expect a pass. Murray saw Neville out of position, saw him stop and try to recover in time, but Murray threw the ball and Desmond, subbing for Phinney, leapt into the air, snatched the ball, and came down falling backward, staying on his feet until Neville made the tackle on the Yale twenty-nine. Three plays later Presley had another chance at a field goal. The ball rose off his toe. It looked good. The Harvard side cheered louder and louder as the ball lofted farther and farther on a line into the wind, loudest as the ball crossed the bar.

A few plays later Yale fumbled again, but Harvard gave back the ball on downs, and the teams traded punts the rest of the quarter.

The teams switched directions. Yale continued to run into the center of the Harvard line without gaining much, and Harvard accomplished very little against Yale. Two hard-hitting teams, Ellsworth wrote. People were getting their money's worth. He scanned the Harvard sideline with his binoculars and saw Felton warming up.

Murray came out and Felton took his position, his uniform bright and clean. He called Casey's number, but the Yale tackle had the play figured out and caught Casey around the knees before he could do one of his shifty changes. Presley tried the center of the line and gained a yard. Felton called his own number, sweeping the Yale end, but the defender grabbed Felton's pads behind his neck and slung him down. Some of the spectators booed. Felton's uniform wasn't clean anymore.

Harvard punted to Yale. Four plays later, Yale punted to Harvard, a short kick, and Harvard took over on the Yale thirty-nine. Havemeyer snapped the ball to Felton. Felton ran forward, stopped suddenly, raised up, and floated the ball over the line. Casey swiped the ball from the air. Like plucking a falling leaf out of the sky. He's running. No one touches him. He runs across the goal and kneels down and presses the ball into the grass and looks up and mugs at the man with a movie camera. Presley added the point.

Late in the half Philip blocked the Yale end and Presley sprinted for a first down, but someone on the line had been holding and the penalty forced Harvard to kick again. Ellsworth marked another punt on his play sheet. Harvard had punted nine times, Yale ten.

At the half, Coach Fisher encouraged the team to hit as hard as they were being hit. If Yale continued to run into the center of the Harvard line, ten points was a strong lead. You've trained hard. You're a hard bunch. You can take anything Yale runs at you, Pooch said.

We're a tired bunch too, Philip thought. He knew Yale's reputation for having talented reserves ready to come in. He knew Kempton could throw the ball as well as could any back in the East. The players trudged out of the locker room.

⁂

The second half begins as a punting game, but Aldrich replaces Neville. Aldrich has fresh legs and a hard, determined look and feints Philip out of position for a gain of twenty yards before Philip and Felton catch up with him. The Yale side is cheering now.

Aldrich again, he spins past Havemeyer and arms Felton out of the way, pushes him aside, but Casey and Presley lunge and tackle his flashing legs.

Third down it's Lay over the middle, faking Sedgwick and almost breaking free. Fourth and one. Havemeyer guesses it's going to be Braden. He squares his shoulders, sheds the block, meets Braden head on. No gain.

Harvard's ball. Casey is caught twice. Presley gains a couple. Harvard punts.

Kempton is tall. Arm like a whip. He sidearms a pass to Walker, a fresh end. Braden charges over Havemeyer, turns, and Kempton slings the ball on target, in the center of Braden's chest, on the blue letters. Braden bulls his way for ten more yards. The Yale fans are waving and cheering. Kempton skips away from Sedgwick and floats the pass to Aldrich again. He turns the wrong way, the ball is over the other shoulder. Philip leaps, comes down with the ball.

But it's Casey for only one, and Presley for one, and Casey again, then a punt. The Harvard side isn't cheering anymore. It senses Yale's relentlessness. Kempton has magic on his side. His passes are bullets. They find their marks. Kempton hands the ball to Lay. He loses it. Recovers it, but the drive has lost its way.

Fourth down, fifty-three yards from the Harvard end zone, the Yale coach waves at Braden to try a field goal. The wind at his back, Braden hits the ball perfectly. It soars into the air at a velocity that stuns everyone. Casey, Presley, Sedgwick stare, mouths open. The Yale players, the crowd, Pooch and Coach Fisher, the other coaches, all silent. The ball crosses the bar with room to spare. Applause crackles from the Yale side.

"We're hanging on. That's about all," Mr. Alston says. The Judge shakes his head.

Through his glasses Mr. Alston finds Philip bent over, exhausted. For a moment he forgets how much he loathes him; for a moment the game is more important than anything else.

Yale is coming down the field again. Twice in a row the Yale end dumps Philip to the ground, hard, punching hits jolting Philip's bones. He stands up. The sky swirls. He shakes his head, refocuses.

Fourth and two. Kempton keeps. Philip sees Kempton's arms going one direction, his legs another. The blocker's shoulder swings into Philip again. He pushes off, keeps his eyes on the blue letters on Kempton's jersey, avoids Kempton's dancing body, the head faking right and left, jams his own shoulder into the quarterback, hears the breath go out of him. They fall together. Once more the Harvard crowd applauds with relief.

But once more Harvard fails to advance the ball. Harvard's punt tumbles into the arms of the Yale receiver forty yards from the Harvard goal.

Yale sends Webb in at half. He and Aldrich alternate. One slashing at Phinney, the other at Philip.

Seven yards from Harvard's goal line now. Five. Three.

Fourth down. Aldrich fakes into the line. Philip recognizes the play, anticipates the lateral to Webb. Rheinhart charges Philip, trying to block him outside to let Webb cut through on the inside. Webb is strong. He prides himself on going inside. Philip knows that, knows how Rheinhart will block, a puncher, a foreman. Philip takes the hit, spins inside, meets Webb off balance, reaches out for Webb's shoe top. Webb falls at the one. Harvard's ball.

Church in to punt for Harvard. The Yale receiver looks up,

loses sight of the ball against the sky, puts out his hands where he thinks the ball will be. The ball thumps against his chest and bounces away. Sedgwick recovers. The receiver bends to one knee and stares at the ground. Yale voices are dying away. People begin to fold their blue blankets and edge toward the exits. Coach Fisher sends in fresh players. The Yale bench glumly watches the game end. Harvard 10. Yale 3.

Grantland Rice sat writing his report: Yale emerged from the stone-age of football just exactly twelve minutes too late. For three quarters the Blue machine hacked grimly away at center and guard. Then Kempton suddenly reverted to a mixture of the rushing, passing game and Harvard escaped a draw and possible defeat by the margin of a gnat's eyelash.

In the locker room Fisher and Pooch embraced the players. Some thought President Lowell would be there to announce his decision. A few waited around, but he didn't appear.

"I'd like to go to California," Coach Fisher said.

"I'm praying for it," Pooch replied.

He was. He leaned forward on his knees and raised his face to the altar in the Church of Peter the Apostle, which he attended every Sunday. I know what I want is trivial, he said, and could not say how much he wanted it or why, only that he did.

~

Philip, showered, dressed, walking toward the Square by himself, changed his mind and returned to the stadium. When he tried to enter through the players' gate, a policeman called out to him.

"Where do you think you're going now?"

Philip hadn't noticed the man. The voice startled Philip. He needed a second to repeat the question to himself and make sense of it.

"I was going in," Philip said.

"You thought you were, but not anyone can walk through the gate, you know."

"But I was just there."

"You played in the game, you mean?"

"Yes. Pratt."

"You're Pratt?" The man squinted at Philip's face. "I can definitely see you got scraped up a bit."

"I hurt all over," Philip said.

"Well . . ." The man's hand was already pushing open the gate. "Go on in. Take your time."

In the early-winter evening the field was nearly dark. Philip remembered running through the fading light at the cottage on the shore, throwing the ball back and forth. Philip remembered Mr. Purdy, what he had told Philip leaving him at the hospital: People black and white will tolerate a carnal relationship between the races; it's love they won't accept. Philip made up his mind to tell Lily.

~

Undefeated. Presley had only one regret. Philip had made the saving tackle. Philip had avoided the reporters. He should at least have been around to shake hands with them, Presley thought as he went from party to party along the Gold Coast, cheered and congratulated with kisses and embraces.

~

Lily didn't want trouble for Walter; she did not ask him to drive her. He offered, though, inquiring where she was going, and concealing his surprise when she told him to Cambridge to a party. Her heavy shoes, trousers, rough shirt, and patched leather jacket impressed Walter as more appropriate for garage work than a party. In her hands she held a thick pair of gloves, the sort a man would wear stoking the furnace, and a helmet like pilots put on, and goggles. Nor did her thoughtfulness seem a party mood. Walter insisted on inspecting the cabbie and the vehicle before wishing Lily good night.

Lily found Philip waiting outside the Hounds, under the striped awning where a masked sultan and Musketeer were smoking cigars and watching the late arrivals, a Marie Antoinette hoisting her skirts to negotiate the exit from her car. Easier from a tumbrel, Lily thought. Hastening around the other side of the car, a Sun King to give Marie his arm.

The goggles hid Lily's eyes. Philip did not recognize her at first. He clutched Lily's hand to steady himself. Embarrassed by his drab costume, he wanted to flee. Uncle Sam had a tear in the trousers. Philip's fur hat, the leather trousers, and shirt were Kit Carson or Daniel Boone or any other frontiersman, vague and recognizable at the same time.

They proceeded through the door. Rooms eerily empty below. Music overhead; the sliding of dancers' feet; saxophone notes trailing down the stairs. That time he found Annette dancing, the Negro musicians, your own people, he remembered her saying. What would Lily say?

Up the stairs, Philip leading Lily by the hand, squeezing by the circumference of a Faerie Queen and dodging a kilted Robert Bruce. Up to the top floor, the glittering ballroom. Chandelier of thirteen stands of light, thousands of bright beads, a hundred candles, and more burning in the sconces. Once the portly Franklin had danced in this glow, now a thin imitator did also, clutching a pink Catherine de'Medici.

Masked couples shifting and turning, and turning and shifting in the mirrors on the walls. Philip and Lily stood and stared. Turbans, scarves, wimples, ruffs, cravats, surcoats, waistcoats, tunics, perukes, trousers, breeches, hose, shirts, pantaloons, boots and shoes and slippers of all kinds; capes, swords, bucklers, bows, arrows, quivers; white hair, blue hair, straight, curled; silks, taffetas, satins, corduroys, velvets; black, green, gray, vermilion, chestnut, fawn, buff all going by; and one tall figure whose head disappeared inside a pumpkin that rested on his shoulders and who out of the circles cut in the orange skin saw and breathed. A Cleopatra, a

Ponce de León, a Robin Hood and a Maid Marian, a Tristram and an Isolde, a Charlie Chaplin, a Sarah Bernhardt, an Oberon danced by. Lily and Philip hid themselves in the crowd.

"There's Es," Lily said.

Philip saw a figure in a yellow chiton sporting a wig of curls encircled by a wreath of tiny white flowers. It was Humphrey with her, they assumed; fur collar, shirt, doublet, jerkin, a dagger dangling from his belt. Humphrey and Esther disappeared behind the Gold Dust twins.

Presley, dressed like Teddy Roosevelt, and Charlotte, in a tunic belted at her waist, a long wig, each strand of orange hair curled into a corkscrew, and bracelets around her wrists, searched over one another's shoulder for an Uncle Sam. The couples danced by each other, Lily's fingers tightening on Philip's arm, but Charlotte did not recognize her.

The band played. The air heated. Couples left to cool themselves downstairs where the waiters mixed Hounds punch. Couples dipped it from bowls using silver cups engraved with the initials of members deceased.

"Some costumes must be the devil to wear," Charlie Chaplin commented to Robin Hood.

"How about holding up a torch all night?"

"Whose torch?" Maid Marian asked, catching the end of Chaplin's remark.

Robin Hood kissed her cheek. "The Statue of Liberty. She went upstairs a minute ago."

Lily heard and guessed. "Let's dance some more," Lily said.

Mina, masked in black, draped in flowing fabrics and wearing a headband with spikes painted to represent light, stood in a corner and watched the dancers. The torch was papier-mâché and she raised it up for several minutes scarcely moving.

"I don't think she's having a very good time," someone said.

"She must want to win a prize awfully much."

The candlelight gave Mina's arms and face a coppery sheen.

The room was full now. Even the waiters wanting to watch who won the prizes had come up. The music stopped. The couples released each other. Ponce de León climbed to the stage and untied his mask. Many of the members yelled for him to put his mask back on. He bowed and managed, doffing his hat, to make an obscene gesture. The members hooted and shouted insults back.

"Now to the prizes. Prize for ladies. And excuse me if I don't get your character exactly right. Mr. Lowell recently reminded me there are some gaps in my education." Pause. A few snickers. "First prize ladies is the Faerie Queen. Come forward and unmask yourself, please."

Through the clapping crowd the Faerie Queen came forth and removed her mask. "Miss Helen Dwight," Ponce de León announced. He kissed Helen's hand as the applause died down.

"Prize for gentlemen." The chant "Teddy, Teddy" began to echo through the room. "Teddy Roosevelt," Ponce de León called out.

The crowd parted to let Presley through. It quieted for a moment as he took off his hat and raised his mask, then cheered loudly some more.

"Prize for couples. Marie and Louis. Which Louis I have no idea."

The couple waved and skipped forward, many in the audience already chanting "Alice," "Wib." They unmasked themselves. "I give you Alice McPherson and Wib Gordon," Ponce de León shouted above the applause.

"Now the grand prize." The audience fell silent again. "The choice was very difficult, but Lady Liberty has honored us with her presence tonight and in return we honor her. The Statue of Liberty."

Applause, subdued now. Some were curious, some envious, some merely bored or too tight or sleepy to concentrate anymore, and a few of the opinion that the winner imposed a solemnity not in the spirit of the event.

Mina took off her mask.

People stared, their eyes scanning her skin. The Gold Dust twins were obviously made up, their honey-toned skin cosmetic. This woman's wasn't. No one said a word. The obvious was not worth one's breath. Silence the cruelest comment. Presley's head shook back and forth. He inhaled short stabs of air.

"I'm Mina Kincaid."

A few applauded, politely, with little enthusiasm. Presley watched the room empty. Somehow minutes had disappeared and he hadn't moved, hadn't been able to keep anything in his mind except Mina. Charlotte was talking to him.

"Do you know her?"

Presley nodded.

Esther was looking for Humphrey. Two people in drab costumes were talking to Mina. Lily kissed Mina's cheek. My God. My God. This can't be, Presley told himself. "Phil, did you bring this woman?"

"I brought Lily."

"Mina, how did you get here?"

"Mr. Rosen."

"Mr. Rosen? I don't know him."

"He's not a member."

"Please leave. I don't wish to see you anymore."

"We're leaving too," Lily said.

The candles had almost burned out. A waxy smoke lingered in the air. Mina, Philip, and Lily were dark figures crossing the room.

"Where will it be then?" Charlotte asked. Presley looked at her blankly. "You and I have to talk."

Presley drove to the Abbots' house. Inside he poured himself a drink. "Fix one for me please," Charlotte said, before leaving Presley by himself.

When Charlotte reappeared, she had changed clothes. She was wearing a green brocade dressing gown that fastened under her chin and hung in pleats to the floor, concealing her almost entirely.

She took the glass he handed her. "I mixed it rather strong," he said, glad to have something to say, hoping to engage her in some conversation other than the one she intended.

"Look. You don't need to explain about that woman to me. But you're damn lucky no one else heard you say you knew her, none of the members. We can keep it all between ourselves."

Presley swallowed and closed his eyes. He replied, "I appreciate your loyalty."

"Loyalty is only one of many things I can give you."

Presley kept his eyes closed and moved his head slightly to tell her he understood. He heard the rustle of her gown. Heard her set her whiskey on the tabletop. Felt her hand on his leg. Presley opened his eyes. Charlotte knelt beside him. He knew her loyalty, her silence, came with a price. He kissed her. She kissed him back, then snuggled contentedly against him.

⁂

Adele Alston watched the street for a car bringing Lily home. Mr. Alston had vanished into the library and shut the door. When he heard Lily's voice, he came out and listened as Mrs. Alston discovered where Lily had been. Mrs. Alston knew who had been with Lily. Philip had kissed her outside. She had witnessed that.

Everet Alston listened as his wife questioned Lily about Mr. Pratt. Lily's calmness betrayed an unrepentant nature. Whatever restrictions Adele imposed on Lily now were too late.

"Why didn't Walter stop you?" Mrs. Alston wondered, weary and ready for sleep.

"Because I wouldn't let him," Lily answered curtly, confirming Mr. Alston's opinion of his daughter's indifference and arrogance. He couldn't touch her; he could reach out, though, and close his fingers around the throat of Philip Pratt. Or perhaps set the dogs on him. That notion pleased Mr. Alston enormously.

On Sunday afternoon Mr. Alston and Mr. Fry met. By evening Mr. Fry was traveling south again.

~

"Come in," Lily said.

"Mother thought you might like a sherry before dinner."

Presley set the glass on the table beside Esther's French book. "I'm not your enemy," he said.

"I prefer to treat you as one."

"Then we should negotiate."

"A peace?"

"A cease-fire."

"Go ahead."

"You and Mina are acquaintances?"

"Friends."

"Let me tell you something about your friend Philip Pratt."

"Are we negotiating?"

"Let's agree we are."

"You're going to reveal Philip's mother was colored."

Presley took a deep breath. "Then there's no point in telling you now, is there? How long have you known?"

"Philip told me last night. If you think my knowing will change my feelings for Philip, you're wrong."

And you're a fool, Presley thought as he beheld his sister. "But Mother and Father don't know, do they?" he said.

Lily sank back in her chair. "I'd prefer they didn't."

"If you agree not to mention my relationship with Mina, I won't tell anyone about Phil."

"Esther went with me to the Bunting."

"It would injure her character to admit that. Make sure she understands."

"I'm sure she does."

"You haven't tasted your sherry."

"Presley, I will say something if you interfere between Philip and me again."

"Then let's promise to stay out of each other's life."

"Promise," Lily said.

On Monday Presley rented rooms in a private house a few doors from the Hounds and hired a man to remove his books and furnishings from Mower.

Most of the students disappeared for the holiday, going home or visiting friends. The Washington was putting on a revival of *Sherlock Holmes*. Jimmy left Philip a ticket at the box office. After the play they went to a cafeteria and ate grilled cheese sandwiches and drank tea. Philip saw an evening paper. The Harvard alumni had convinced President Lowell to send the team to California. Harvard had accepted an invitation to play in the Tournament of Roses game on New Year's Day.

"Maybe you'll have your picture taken with Douglas Fairbanks," Jimmy said. "Did that guy try to get any money for the picture of you handing out food?"

Philip shook his head.

Jimmy slapped Philip on the back. "Probably understood you were a deadbeat to begin with."

"Did you believe all the things you said, Jimmy?"

"Phil, didn't you know? I was hired to act. I was pretty convincing, wasn't I?" Jimmy lit a cigarette. At another table a man in a shabby Ulster coat crumbled crackers into a bowl of soup. "To be honest, I believe what I said, but not the way I said it."

They finished their coffee. "You'll see Lily again, Phil. I'm sure you will," Jimmy said to cheer up Philip.

Only a few lights in the windows in the Yard, one in Professor Copeland's room in Hollis. His window was open and Phil could hear the words and knew Copey was walking back and forth reciting poetry in the room where once Emerson had suffered a winter so cold that each morning he broke ice in a pan for water to wash with. But Lily warmed Philip. She didn't say it didn't matter when he told her about his mother. It does matter, she said. She forgave him for not telling her sooner. I will go where you go, she said. You have only to ask. Only to love me.

⁂

After the Thanksgiving holiday, Mr. Alston summoned Presley to the library and closed the door. He explained hiring Mr. Fry. Presley didn't believe Phil had anything to do with the missing car, but he understood how his father had interpreted the circumstances.

Then Mr. Alston detailed other events: the fatal beating of a Negro named Purdy, the wounding of a policeman, Philip's presence. Mr. Fry's reason for Philip being there Presley knew was wrong, but he didn't doubt Philip was in trouble. Best let Mr. Fry do his job and keep the agreement with Lily: Say nothing about Philip, stay out of her life.

"Mr. Fry has talked to the policeman. He's eager for Mr. Pratt to return to Charleston at Christmas. He recommends dealing with Mr. Pratt privately. Money is involved, of course. Money always is," Mr. Alston said.

"It would be useful," he added, "if Mr. Pratt indicated when he might return home."

⁂

Pooch caught up with Philip in Harvard Square. Casey had made Camp's All-American. "You're All-East," Pooch said. "Are you packed for California?"

"I'm not going," Philip answered.

Pooch gripped Philip's arm. "What are you talking about?"

"I'm not going. My season's over."

"You've started every game."

"Malone will do a good job. You'll see."

"Tell me what's wrong."

"Nothing's wrong. Believe me."

Pooch watched Philip walk away.

⁂

Noon sparkling under the hemlocks. Girls teased each other and fingered initials and hearts into the snow beside the path.

"Charlotte will drop you in the Square," Esther said.

She was aloof now. Something was happening between Charlotte and Presley. Esther was sworn to secrecy. Presley had invited Charlotte to all the Christmas parties.

Charlotte drove to Cambridge. Beside her, Esther read a book. In back, Lily watched out the window.

Lily ascended the steps to Philip's room. She knocked. The door opened. Philip lifted her in his arms.

He laid her down. She inhaled the heat of the fire. Philip kissed the warmth on her skin. "It's all right," she said. "It's all right. Don't stop."

Lily had read the copy of *What Every Girl Should Know* that her mother had given her, but Mina had told Lily what to do. It hurt, but not very much, and not for very long. "Darling, darling, thank you," she said in Philip's arms.

In the fire's glow she told Philip what she had found in her father's desk, how easy the lock opened. "I've done it for ages," she said. "My father hired a man called Fry to find out things about you. There's a list of names, people in Charleston. Mr. Purdy, a black man, who was killed in his house. A wounded policeman who saw a white man kill Mr. Purdy. And someone who drove you to the station. Who are they?" Lily asked.

Who would believe anything he had to say except Lily? What were his chances? Philip began the story, told her as much as he knew and guessed the rest. The other policeman he'd seen in the doorway had found the wounded man in Mr. Purdy's room. Philip didn't say Mr. Purdy's death was his fault, but he knew it was, and would know it forever.

Philip lay beside Lily again. He saw himself stepping down from the train in Charleston. Would he recognize the men waiting for him? Would one have a scar on his throat? Would Mr. Fry be with them? And where will they take me? he wondered. To what hidden place? He would lose more than a toe this time. Mr. Purdy's prophecy would finally come true.

"I can't go home," Philip said. "I don't know where I'll go."

He walked with Lily to Massachusetts Avenue. "I promise to write after Christmas," he said. A cab stopped for her. He stood by the gate. She waved good-bye and got in.

⁂

Presley knocked. Philip opened the door.

"Word's out you quit the team."

"That's one way to look at it."

"I didn't take you for a quitter."

Philip arched his brows. "Didn't Annette tell you? I assumed she told you all about me."

"Your secrets are safe with me, Phil. Anyway, you're only part Negro. The wrong part, in her opinion."

"What's your opinion? One drop of Negro blood changes you completely?"

"I'm not here to discuss what I believe."

"But that's what you think?"

"What if I do?"

"I'm not surprised, but I'm disappointed. I hoped you were a different person. So did Mina."

"Who cares what she thinks. I got my money's worth."

"If you were buying humiliation, you did. You really looked foolish."

Philip saw Presley's hand tighten. When he swung, Philip pushed Presley's fist away.

"Don't do that again," Philip said.

Presley straightened his jacket.

"You're not worth it anyway," he said.

"Then why are you here?" Philip asked.

"Since you aren't going with the team to California, I wondered if you were going home."

The question Philip had expected. "I plan to return to Charleston on the twenty-first."

"I suppose you'll see Lily before you leave."

"Are you here about Lily, then?"

"I have no interest in Lily anymore. That's not why I'm here." Presley drew a silver flask out of his coat pocket. "Let's have a final drink."

Philip handed Presley a glass. It slipped through his fingers and shattered on the floor. He bent down to pick up the pieces. He didn't notice the small cut at first. Philip found another glass and Presley poured out some whiskey.

Presley raised his glass. "To the team," he said and touched his glass against Philip's.

Philip saw the ring of blood on Presley finger.

"You're cut," he said.

"I'll wash it off." Presley put down his glass.

"Wait."

Philip squeezed a shard of glass between his fingers and wiped the palm of his other hand across the edge.

"Now we're both bleeding." Presley sounded as if everything was too tiresome.

Philip had no doubt what Presley would do next, when Philip offered his hand, but he needed to make Presley do it.

"Brothers," Philip said, guiding Presley's finger to his hand to press their flesh together.

Presley yanked his hand away. "Never," he said.

Presley disappeared into the bathroom and returned with a towel pressed against his cut.

"I always heal fast," Presley said. He picked up his glass, swallowed the whiskey, put down the glass, opened the door, closed the door behind him.

"Don't count on it," Philip said.

~ ~ ~

Blue afternoon in the South. December 21. Along the Battery carriage rides. The pop of firecrackers. In the station voices announcing trains hollowly. The trains from Washington arrive. Mr. Fry and two policemen watch the passengers getting off. No Philip Pratt. All evening they watch, the next day, and the next.

"You'll get paid, at least" Mr. Fry says, "I'll see to that. Mr. Alston will need to think the work is done."

"We can convince him," one of the policemen says. "But we'll want extra for the coroner," the other says.

"The matter has been taken care of," Mr. Fry telegrams to Mr. Alston.

Christmas. Presents for the servants. Lily has chosen a silk scarf for Walter. It pleases him.

"You're eighteen tomorrow," Mrs. Alston said. "Lily, what would you like?"

A letter, a letter, Lily thinks.

"Your father and I discussed a trip to London next summer."

"Fine. Fine," Lily says. A letter, a letter, she thinks.

Philip sailed from New Orleans. "I am in Barbados. I love you," he writes.

Lily's letter is addressed to her school. The safest place to send it, Philip believes. Miss Prentice tucks the letter away. When will Lily come back? Miss Prentice is old now. She forgets. She finds the letter weeks afterward. She intends to give it to Lily but will forget again and lose it again.

Presley departs for California. The early winter along the middle route is severe. Drifting snow blocks the train. Ellsworth writes copy about players running up and down the coaches or causing chaos in the Pullmans. In Wyoming the team gets off the train and practices formations on the main street of Green River under the shadow of mountains, the players high-stepping across snow, the local rabble, full of whiskey, cheering them on.

"This arrived in the mail today."

NAME OF DECEASED: Philip Lanier Pratt. The document on onion skin signed by the coroner; City of Charleston, County of Charleston, South Carolina, December 27, 1919.

"I'll go tell Lily," Adele Alston says.

California. A party at the home of Douglas Fairbanks. Charlie Chaplin attends and Zasu Pitts. Tours of studios. Flirtations. Everywhere the scent of flowers, and heat more than easterners are accustomed to. The players from Oregon are used to it. They will wear the easterners down, Ellsworth writes.

~

Weeks after the game, an American newspaper is left behind by a guest at the hotel where Philip has found work. He sits at his table, the sun aslant through the blinds, a lizard traversing the dust under the window.

Philip flattens the paper with his palm. "Against formidable odds the team from the East outscored the team from the West. Although Oregon took first advantage on a drop kick by Steers, Harvard marched down the field on runs by Casey and passes by Murray. Freddy Church, substituting for Presley Alston, injured early in the contest, faked a kick and sprinted twelve yards for a touchdown. Ted Malone kicked the point. Shortly before the second period ended, Clifford Manerud, substitute quarter, drop-kicked another Oregon goal. Harvard led 7 to 6 and its defense, despite the heat and attacks from the Oregon line, held the slim advantage. Harvard finished with a 78-yard drive of its own that ended on the Oregon 1 on the final play of the game."

Boats come and go. Every morning Philip sorts the mail. No letters with his name. He decides to stay on. Heat agrees with him. Sometimes he goes to the tidy schoolroom near the grounds of the hotel. Shutters are open. Sun pours in. He reads to the children from a book of Poe. The children concentrate, their brown faces full of delight. The words, the rhymes, the meter, how they love them. "Ulalume," Philip says, and the children hum "Ulalume. Ulalume." When Philip quotes *The Raven* the children giggle and clap. "Nevermore. Nevermore," he says. "Nevermore. Nevermore," they chorus in return.

Nevermore. Nevermore. Philip grieves for Lily. Her smile, her voice, her eyes, how he misses her.

~

Lily grieves. No letter. Why? She has never felt so empty, so lost.

A jumble of weeks goes by. She delays returning to school until February. Voices surround her. She listens but cannot hear. Hears but cannot understand. She lives in the dark, in the theater where other people's stories go in and out of focus. *Broken Blossoms,* Lily has seen it dozens of times.

~

In the years ahead Lily and Mina will become great friends They will walk arm and arm, Lily often attired in a fine suit of men's clothes cut especially for her. There will be an outrageous kiss, Lily and Mina on a spring afternoon on Newbury Street, that Charlotte Alston will witness. She will say nothing about it to Presley. Charlotte and Presley speak little to each other.

Presley served in the embassy in Athens, his tour marred by certain incidents and compromises, certain women expensive to keep out of sight. "Not reliable" is the ambassador's judgment of Presley's character.

Presley returns to Boston. None of his business ventures ends well. He always needs money. He is unwelcome at the Hounds now, and if he decides to attend a football game on a golden autumn afternoon, scarcely anyone speaks to him. Once he encounters Ellsworth buying a cigar. Ellsworth nods and walks away.

Lily will buy a house close to the one she grew up in, the one on Louisburg Square that her mother will sell after her father dies. A stroke in a taxi coming home from an evening of cards, coming home full of whiskey and silence and disappointment, coming home to the painting he commissioned (he wanted Sargent, but Sargent declined): Presley in his uniform, a pistol holstered on his belt. How much money has he given Presley to settle debts and silence rumors? After the funeral, Mrs. Alston will choose to live the rest of her days in the cottage on the shore.

Lily will share her house with Mina. They will give marvelous parties and have many lovers. Despite hard times, Lily's money will last. She will write stories and publish them in magazines under different names. Philip will read one or two and not know who wrote them.

The cottage, the house on the shore, how Presley will desire it. He's lost everything else. On a July morning in 1935, Mrs. Alston departs this life. The cottage belongs to him, except for some furniture, the attorney cautions, and one set of the silver. Also this stipulation: If Lily should have children, they shall inherit the cottage after Presley's lifetime. Lily gazes into the halo of light where the sun glows around the curtain drawn across the attorney's window to cool the room. In her memory she sees Philip for the first time. She has never stopped loving him.

Summer passes. Lily has no wish to spend another winter in Boston. Mina's lover has invited her to accompany him to Cairo. You're invited too, Mina says. I think I'll try a cruise, Lily says.

The boat stops in Barbados. Lily disembarks wearing white trousers and jacket and a straw hat with a soft brim. Seated in the bar at the Reef Club where Philip works she removes her hat. Her hair is cut short and for a moment the waiter, noticing her collar and neckwear, mistakes her for a man. Must think she's George Sand or something, the waiter remarks in Philip's hearing. Philip decides to have a look.

Lily sips her drink. Glancing up, she sees Philip in the doorway. Her mouth falls open. She gapes at Philip; he at her. He scarcely feels the floor under his feet as he stumbles toward her. The world rearranges itself. Lily rises, rises to meet him, rises to open her arms, rises to embrace him, to be embraced. They hold each other. The room is full of startled visitors who do not comprehend the histories of these two people, but what they see before them, this man and woman delighting in each other as if they had been newly created, appears so spontaneous and wonderful that someone begins to clap and soon everyone is applauding.

That night they lay in each other's arms in a small room by the sea. Wouldn't it be lovely, Lily said, if we could have a child. She already knew that was going to happen.

~

Sometime after he arrived on the island, Philip can't remember exactly when, he started another letter, writing it in his head, like the ones he tried to write before to tell Presley about Annette. This letter begins, *Presley, I loved you long before I loved your sister.* The letters ends, *Do you remember that evening after the party at the house on the shore? We threw the ball to each other until the light was gone from the sky. You were handsome and brave and I would have believed anything you told me. Now I have this to tell you. Light is always entering the dark or disappearing from it. Day is in night. Night is in day. To discern something so obvious has taken me a long time, but it is one of the only truths I know.*

I acknowledge the influence on this work of John Dos Passos's *1919*, George Weller's *Not to Eat, Not for Love*, and *The Black Notebooks* by Toi Derricotte.

I acknowledge my gratitude to Geoffrey Movius, David Morcom, and, above all, Ann Page Stecker.

Finally, I wish to thank the Rev. Canon Harold B. Sedwick, for his charm and his memories of Cambridge.

Book design by Dean Bornstein